WULFIE
STAGE FRIGHT

WULFIE
STAGE FRIGHT

Lindsay J Sedgwick
Illustrated by Josephine Wolff

Little Island Books

WULFIE: STAGE FRIGHT

First published in 2020 by

Little Island Books

7 Kenilworth Park

Dublin 6W

Ireland

Text © Lindsay J Sedgwick 2020

Illustrations © Josephine Wolff 2020

The Author has asserted her moral rights.

ISBN: 978-1-912417-45-2

Illustrated by Josephine Wolff

Designed by Catherine Gaffney

Edited by Venetia Gosling

Copy-edited and proofread by Emma Dunne

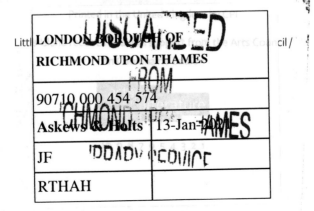

For my daughter, Libby. May her dreams come true.

Chapter 1

As Libby climbed up to her room, the shadows shifted. They came out of nooks and crannies and open cupboard doors. They stretched across the floor, slid down the stairs and lapped at her feet. It was an old, odd house, each staircase narrower and darker than the last, and right at the very top, so far up it was impossible to go any further without climbing onto the roof, was Libby's bedroom.

She had just snuggled into her bed underneath the skylight when Rex burst in.

'I'm going to tell you a bedtime story,' he said. 'And it's going to make you cry.'

Oh dear, thought Libby.

Her brother – step-brother, really – jumped up onto Libby's bed and had a practice bounce. Rex was small and mean, but Libby was smaller and Rex was very good at telling stories that made her cry.

Being hidden in the eaves, full of corners and dark spaces, Libby's room was the perfect place in which to scare little sisters. She pulled her legs to one side before he stood on them. Chilly air reached in and tickled her toes.

So now she was cold, as well as hungry and scared.

'Ms Emily in drama class says I've to practise my storytelling skills,' said Rex.

The bed rocked precariously. It only had three proper legs. The fourth was made from a pile of books. Sometimes Libby took one of the books to bed and slept at an angle.

The moonlight lit up Rex's scruffy red hair, making him look more medium-sized monster than small boy.

'I think Veronika just called you,' Libby said in a tiny voice. Veronika was Rex's mum.

'Oh, she can wait.' Rex grinned. He had a smudge of chocolate on his nose. 'We went for chocolate sundaes while you were cleaning the house.' He bent down over her and scrunched up his face. 'You can lick my nose if you like.'

A drop of snot landed exactly above where her mouth would have been if Libby hadn't yanked a corner of her duvet up extra quickly.

'Suit yourself.' Rex licked his nose clean. 'Remember the Big Bad Wolf?'

She remembered. Rex's Big Bad Wolf was nothing like the one in the book of fairy tales in the school library. *His* Big Bad Wolf was enormously hairy and ate little girls. Slowly. Starting with their toes. Or sometimes he'd just have a finger or two in a sandwich with some mayonnaise.

And he never ate boys, according to Rex.

The moon slid silently behind a cloud that was as long and thin as a panini. Libby's tummy rumbled. She wondered if chocolate sundaes tasted nice. She'd had a square of chocolate once. It had only lasted long enough for her to want more.

Rex cleared his throat and began. 'Once upon a time there was this little girl ...'

Libby tuned out by staring through the skylight, imagining what it would be like on the moon. The moon moved out from behind the cloud-panini but stayed silent. She thought it might be cold, like her feet.

One day she would take all the books that held up her bed, learn the maps that were inside them and have adventures of her own, away from Rex. They were books with leather covers, emblazoned with the name that was also carved into the big trunk in the corner that smelled of the sea: *Zebediah F Flanagan*. Her great-great-grandfather.

Her father said the *F* stood for *Fearless* and she believed him.

Libby wanted to be fearless. She had curly blonde hair that never stayed in a plait but was just about okay in pigtails. She'd never heard of explorers with pigtails so she would have to be the first.

Rex's words seeped into her ears.

'... they yanked her into the graveyard, where the Big Bad Wolf, all scraggly nightfall ...' Rex paused. He liked the phrase. His mother had made him learn it off by heart so he'd sound intelligent. '... was chasing the little girl. The ground slid under her feet. Full of holes and bones and dead bodies heaving and goo and gore and eyeballs popping out of the mud ...'

Libby closed her eyes.

'No matter how fast she ran, the little girl – who looks *exactly* like you, Libby – could never get away.'

Libby could hear their parents talking downstairs. A hum (Dad) interspersed with crackling (Veronika). *I might as well be on a different planet,* she thought, gazing through the skylight. *Or a star. A beautiful, warm and friendly star where big brothers don't exist.*

'The Big Bad Wolf's eyes bored into her head. He was sharpening his claws on the gravestones as he followed her. "I'm going to gobble you up," he said.'

'Why doesn't he eat boys?' said Libby.

The shadows in the room were getting too big. The trunk that smelled of the sea was casting a shadow she knew would creep up the wall, across the ceiling and down onto her bed. It was Rex's doing. His story would make it happen.

She made herself look at her step-brother. 'Is it because they're stinky like you?'

Rex jumped onto the floor with a thud. 'Everyone knows the Big Bad Wolf only eats girls. They're the pointless ones.'

'We are *not*!'

If she could get him to talk about how much he hated girls, he might forget to finish his story. They never ended well.

But Rex smiled and wiped his runny nose on Libby's duvet. 'She couldn't run fast enough,' he went on. 'She was small and stupid and only just ten so she ran the wrong way, down to the narrow end of the graveyard, until there was only one grave left. A grave that had the biggest and scariest tomb, shaped just like *that*!' Rex pointed into the darkest corner of Libby's room. At the trunk. 'Full of skulls. Rats.'

Libby gulped and tried to count backwards in sevens from a hundred in her head.

'Oh, he slowed down now, the Big Bad Wolf. He slowed down and licked his lips at the thought of the meal ahead.'

Seventy-nine. Seventy-two. Sixty-five. Fifty-eight.

'She backed into the tomb and as the wolf stretched out a claw ...'

Thirty-seven. Thirty. Twenty-three.

Rex leant down over her head. 'Slowly, the lid of the tomb opened.'

Libby tried not to open her eyes. She had a story to write for school about Granuaile, the pirate queen from Galway in the West of Ireland. They'd studied her in class. If Libby concentrated on working out what she'd write in her head, maybe it would stop Rex's words getting in there. Granuaile would help her to be brave.

'*Creeeaak,*' said Rex, wriggling his fingers in the air.

Libby's eyes popped open, all of their own accord. In the corner, the trunk was rattling.

As if there was something inside.

Rex didn't notice. 'The stench of rotting flesh flooded out,' he said, relishing every word.

The front door opened downstairs and Libby heard her father dragging the bins through the house to put them out front. *Granuaile. Pirates. Galway Bay. Rattling trunk.*

'"I'm going to drag you into my tomb," the wolf said. "I'm going to pluck off your toes and eat them one by one.'" Rex made a slurping sound. Libby ducked under the covers. "'I'll dip them in ketchup and have them for tea—'"

'Rexipoo!' called Veronika's voice.

At last, thought Libby.

'You still upstairs?'

By the time Veronika stepped into the room, Rex was standing by the door with tears in his eyes. (He was practising tears-on-demand for Ms Emily's drama class.)

'What's wrong, darling?' asked Veronika.

Rex looked up at his mum with big wet eyes. 'Libby said my story was rubbish!'

'That's hardly a nice thing to say, Libby!'

Libby's head popped out from under the covers. 'B-but—!'

'Look at you, all warm and cosy in bed, and your brother making this huge effort to come up four flights of stairs to tell you a bedtime story!'

Rex stuck his tongue out at Libby, so she did it back. Trouble was, Veronika was facing her at the time.

'Libby! Apologise to your brother and say thank you.'

'Thank you, Rex,' said Libby, keeping an eye on the now-silent trunk at the end of the room. Had it really rattled?

The thing was, everything Rex said, Veronika believed. Everything Libby said, Veronika disbelieved. It was that simple.

And Rex was a *lot* better at lying than Libby.

They were both ten years old, with only a few months between them, but Libby's own mother had been mislaid when Libby was very young, while Rex's mother had found Libby's dad when Libby was nearly four and a half. Veronika had hoped he'd become a famous inventor someday and make them all rich but he hadn't managed it yet.

To get Libby's dad, Veronika had had to take on Libby too. But it seemed she only had enough love to spare for one child.

Rex.

'My poor generous boy,' Veronika said now. 'What story were you telling her?'

'The Big Bad Wolf in the graveyard.'

'Oh, yes. Nice. Lots of *nibble nibble, crunch crunch*?'

'I was just getting to that part,' said Rex.

Rex's mum clicked each of her fingers with their long purple fingernails and smiled at her son. 'Always good to leave something to the imagination,' she said.

As Veronika ushered Rex out, Libby asked in a little voice, 'Could you leave the light on, please?'

'Don't be ridiculous!' said Veronika. 'You have the moon to light up your room.' Rex had three nightlights *and* two big windows facing the street in his room. 'It's not as if the Big Bad Wolf actually *lives* in our attic,' Veronika went on. 'Though, if he *was* to live somewhere, your room does have the right atmosphere, with that smelly old trunk. It's probably full of skulls.'

'That's what I said!' Rex beamed.

'You know, Libby, fear is a smell the Big Bad Wolf particularly likes,' said Veronika. 'The more afraid you are, the more likely it is that he'll appear and gobble you up while you're sleeping.'

'Mum!' said Rex. 'You're a genius. I wish I'd thought of that.'

Then they left Libby there, in her little bed at the top of the house, and they chuckled all the way downstairs.

As Libby's bedroom door clicked shut, the moon slipped silently behind a large cloud shaped just like the face of a wolf, with teeth sharp as claws.

Chapter 2

'I don't know why Rex can't make his own breakfast and lunch,' Libby said the next morning as she buttered slices of bread in the kitchen. She hadn't slept much but she'd already put on a wash, made the beds and hoovered the stairs.

'Because he walks you to school,' said Veronika. 'That sandwich is far too small for Rex. Give him yours as well.'

'But then I only have an apple!'

'Which will teach you not to make small sandwiches for a growing boy.'

—

School was a short walk away, across two busy roads, one small green and a long block of houses with different coloured doors. It was winter, with wind so hard it planted minuscule icicles under your fingernails.

Or under Libby's fingernails, at least, since Rex had calf-skin, fur-lined gloves.

Libby could see the Spire stretching up over the rooftops from the centre of Dublin city. It was taller than everything – 120 metres high – and made from a shiny metal so it would reflect the city and its visitors.

Rex had told her that it stole reflections: 'Once the Spire has your reflection, it traps it inside forever so it can gobble your soul.'

But he was wrong. Libby had gone on a school trip to town and the Spire had only captured her reflection for a moment. She'd looked back as they left, just in case, but it was already reflecting the flower-seller nearby.

What Libby's step-mother didn't know was that Libby had been going to school by herself for years. Every morning, Rex abandoned her for his gang right around the corner. They could push and punch and trip each other and talk sports all the way to school and they did *not* want girls anywhere near.

Libby didn't mind walking alone. She could wave to the cats in the windows – there were six – and pet the dogs in gateways, watching the kids going to school. Her favourite was a dog called Sasuke. He was a muddle of a dog, with ears and feet and colouring from all sorts of breeds, but his fur was soft and warmed her hands.

(Today, Rex told his mates the story he'd told Libby the previous night. Instead of being frightened, his friends laughed. Rex didn't like being laughed at, so he hung back and caught Libby stroking Sasuke.)

'You know how the Big Bad Wolf *loves* the smell of fear? Well, he eats dogs *all* the time,' said Rex. He thought his mother would be proud of him for thinking of this. 'If the Big Bad Wolf smells dog on you, he won't be able to stop himself gobbling you all up.'

Libby stopped stroking the dog and put her hands in her pockets.

Sasuke looked sad.

(Another boy, new to their school, was passing just then, humming a tune in his head. Nazim was tall and thin with a flounce of hair that bounced as he walked. He had glasses so thick you could use them to light fires

from sticks made of snow. He watched Libby as she put her head down and ran all the way to the school gates and into class, and wondered why every school he went to *had* to have bullies.)

—

Libby and Rex were in the same class. The principal of the school believed it was a good idea to keep families together. In this case, the principal was very much mistaken. Libby sat up near the front and tried to learn. Rex sat two rows back and tried to hit her with pencils. If she moved quickly in and out of class, she could usually avoid him until home time.

Libby didn't have any real friends at school because every time she made a friend Rex was mean to them too. Libby didn't blame them for leaving her alone.

'Silence!' Their teacher, Ms Poddle, held up a hand and the classroom hushed. 'Great and exciting news! Our school is going to put on its first ever play – a play that has been written by me – for one night only.'

Up on the blackboard, Ms Poddle wrote the title: *The Big Bad Wolf.*

Libby sat up straight, a shiver running down her spine. School was the one place she'd thought she'd be free of the Big Bad Wolf.

But then Ms Poddle finished the title: ... *Learns His Lesson.*

Libby grinned. She hadn't thought wolves could learn lessons. She had always wanted to be in a play, and she loved the idea of being in one where the Big Bad Wolf was punished for being bad.

'All proceeds will go to building a better enclosure for the wolves at the zoo,' Ms Poddle said. 'If you would like to be in the play, and be part of something truly amazing, add your name to the page that will be posted up on the main noticeboard tomorrow. Auditions will be held after school in two days' time. Unfortunately, those who get roles will miss out on some classes for the next few weeks.'

The room buzzed with chatter. Libby sat still and dreamt.

She dreamt all the way through maths – of lights around a mirror in a dressing room and a star on the door that read: *Libby Lou's Room.*

She dreamt all the way through break-time – seeing herself on stage, moving everyone to tears and laughter. She dreamt of big bunches of flowers.

In Art, Ms Poddle got them to draw posters to advertise the play. Libby decided that hers would have a border of wolves in different poses and the title would be made out of tiny pigs playing piggyback, with hammers and nails for building houses.

Art was over too soon, so Libby dreamt her way to lunchtime. Of Veronika sitting in the front row, clapping and clapping till the tips of her fingers went pink, her smile only for Libby, her eyes lit up and her lips saying, for all the world to hear, 'That's our Libby. Isn't she amazing?'

'Hey, dimbot! You're blocking the door!'

Libby blinked at the harsh lights of the school corridor and then up at Rex.

'I said move, muskrat!'

Libby shifted sideways and Rex pushed past, bumping and pinching her at the same time. She made her way out into the yard and over to the farthest corner where she slipped in behind an old oak tree. This was her safe space. Rex never went near the tree. He was afraid squirrels would throw acorns at him or birds would poop on his perfectly fluffy hair.

Besides, nobody could see him being mean if he was hidden behind a tree. Rex liked to display his meanness openly.

Libby sat down under her favourite branch, ate her lunchtime apple quietly and tried to think of other things.

Chapter 3

'Do I *have* to go?' Rex dragged his feet down the stairs, stopping in the hall to shake crumbs from the biscuit he was eating onto the floorboards Libby was polishing.

'Yes,' said Veronika, 'you do.' She handed him his coat.

Rex had been going to Ms Emily's Academy of Drama and Dance and Doing Good Things for three years now. Veronika and Libby's dad always went to watch because Veronika thought her son was a genius.

Libby was less sure.

'Where's your other glove?' said Veronika.

'Oh, I gave it to Libby,' said Rex. 'Her hands were cold. She's probably lost it since.'

'My darling selfless boy. Hear that, Jack?' she said to Libby's dad. 'Now, Libby – the glove, if you please!'

'He never –'

'There you go, lying again,' said Veronika. 'No supper for you tonight.'

Libby never got supper so it wasn't much of a loss.

—

Once upon a time, Libby had asked, 'Can't I go to drama classes too?'

Her step-mother had laughed. 'Don't be ridiculous. You need *talent*! Do you have talent?'

'I might have,' Libby had said. She'd been feeling brave.

'Rubbish. You are nothing but an irritating mouse.'

'Now, my dearest,' Dad had said. 'Mice don't set out to be irritating. They're only living their lives the way nature intended –'

The look Veronika had given Dad sent him scurrying outside, 'to get the car warmed up'.

—

Ms Emily had once been a child star in films. She would have been Anakin Skywalker in *Star Wars* only the director discovered she was a girl at the final audition. There were photos of Ms Emily in full costume all along the walls of her academy, which was in an old building in the city centre. They showed her as Oliver and Madeline and Stuart Little, all by the age of twelve.

Veronika occasionally allowed Libby to tag along and admire Rex's acting genius. Libby didn't think Rex was very good. She always had his lines memorised while he was still getting them wrong. She could pull her face into all sorts of expressions while his remained locked into one. When she wasn't memorising home-work as she did her chores, Libby ran over the scenes she'd seen Ms Emily's students perform and played all the parts in turn.

'I was going to bring you with us today,' said Veron-ika now, 'but your deplorable behaviour to your brother last night has forced me to leave you behind.' She checked her appearance in the hall mirror. *God, but I am beautiful,* she thought. 'I was even hoping to take you for your first ever ice-cream sundae afterwards AND hot chocolate made with real melted chocolate, topped with cream and little tiny pieces of toffee.'

'I don't think you were, really,' said Libby and she started upstairs.

'Stop right there, you ungrateful little brat!'

Libby stopped halfway up the first flight of stairs. She had been aiming to reach the third stair from the top, having decided quite a long time ago that the third stair from the top was her lucky step on any set of stairs. She turned slowly.

'You want me to tell the Big Bad Wolf to come and eat you?' said Veronika.

Libby felt a small icy finger slide down her back.

'Maybe I'll send him a text right now. Tell him to come and get you while we're out.'

Rex snorted. 'Good one, Mum.'

'I wouldn't be at all surprised if we came home to find you all gobbled up, with lots of slobber.' Veronika pulled on her snakeskin gloves. 'The Big Bad Wolf is always on the lookout for nasty, naughty little girls who take up too much space and lose gloves.' She turned on her heels. 'Come along, Rexipoo!'

Rex flicked a little snot at Libby and followed Veronika out.

Libby's father pulled on his coat and hat and looked up at Libby. His eyes were green and sympathetic. 'Sorry, Mouse,' he said, running up to pat her on the head. 'You really shouldn't upset her so.'

'But I didn't DO anything,' said Libby as the front door snapped shut.

She sat on the stairs and tried not to feel sad.

'Like I'm even scared,' she said.

And shivered.

Chapter 4

'Dunno why the Big Bad Wolf can't eat little boys,' Libby muttered to herself. 'Rex is lots naughtier than me and he lies *all* the time. If the Big Bad Wolf hates naughtiness so much, you'd think he'd sniff it out, as if it was chocolate sauce or gravy or something.'

On the third stair before her bedroom door, Libby had an idea.

A brave sort of idea, full of fluffiness and oompf.

She was tired of being scared. Completely and utterly weary of it. If she found the Big Bad Wolf herself, she wouldn't have to be scared any more. He might eat her up, which was definitely a possible flaw in the plan, but perhaps Libby could persuade him to feast on Rex first, with his mother for seconds ...

That'd teach them to be mean to her.

Libby went to her room and pulled on her favourite thing. It was a big blue jumper that went down to her knees and had holes in the sleeves which were handy for putting her thumbs through. It had been her mother's, Dad said. Then she went looking.

First, she looked in the ordinary hiding places. She peeked in the cupboards under the stairs for yellow eyes and slavering jaws. She checked every corner of the kitchen, the dining room, the sitting room, the laundry room, the ironing room, the scullery and the hall.

Then she unlocked the cellar door and stopped, chewing her hair.

'There are dead bodies in the cellar,' Rex had once said, 'glued to the wall with human hair. Nobody knows who they are or where they came from. Every few years, they grab someone new to take their place.'

'Cellar,' she said aloud, 'I'm tired of being scared.'

Still, before she went down the steps, Libby wedged the door open with an old boot and flicked on the light. She held on tight to the stair-rail in case she needed to flee. The cellar was full of old bikes, a toilet bowl and wonky furniture. A sharp wind squeezed in through a broken window high up in the wall, running its fingers through some old Hallowe'en costumes hanging on an old lamp. Something squidgy oozed between Libby's toes and a couple of mice squeaked at her for stepping on their dinner. She backed into a dressmaker's dummy and screamed. Malachy, the neighbour's cat, who had just crept in the broken window, fled up the stairs in search of a warm place to sleep.

After the cellar, she worked her way up through the rest of the house. She looked in wardrobes and under beds, and eventually she ended up back in her attic bedroom, staring at the only place she hadn't checked.

Zebediah F Flanagan's trunk.

'He locked himself inside to escape from pirates but nobody remembered to ever let him out ...' Rex had once said.

Last night, it had been a tomb full of skulls and rats.

Libby pondered the trunk from all sides. It didn't seem large enough for a dead body or a Big Bad Wolf, but there was nowhere else in the house the wolf could be. She leant down and whispered to the trunk: 'Before I let you out, promise me you'll eat Rex first!' There wasn't any reply, so Libby began to turn the key. It was stiff. She thought it might snap but then it turned with a loud, echoey crunching sound. Like teeth on bones.

Outside, rain clouds replaced the pale winter sun.

Libby took a deep breath, crossed her fingers behind her back and used both hands to lift the lid. A smell of sea salt and seaweed wafted out but nothing grabbed her and dragged her in.

She lifted out a torn leather waistcoat. A hat with broken peacock feathers. A snakeskin purse full of coins.

No dead bodies. No skeletons. No wolves of any size or badness.

Her hand went down and down and she filled her bedroom floor with items from the trunk.

A red velvet cape, floor-length and patched. A pack of playing cards that smelled of owls. Black boots with toes that curled up.

A broken lamp. A map. A compass.

A pair of baggy trousers. A shirt with ruffles. A real stuffed rabbit, with only one eye, mounted on a plinth.

How could so much fit into the trunk when it still seemed full?

Libby peered inside, careful to hold onto the sides in case she fell in.

And there, right down in the darkness, at the bottom of the trunk, she saw a pair of yellow eyes.

Which blinked.

Chapter 5

Libby jumped back and landed on her bum halfway across the room, her breath catching in her throat. There was something in the trunk. It had eyes the colour of mustard and fur as thick as the darkest night. She thought she had seen a snout and ears.

Libby closed her eyes, counted to ten and walked over to peep inside the trunk again.

Whatever was inside the trunk was trying to look, as far as Libby could tell, like a furry duvet. But Libby knew it wasn't a duvet because duvets don't have ears.

She blinked and looked again. Now it was a coat made out of purple fur – but coats don't have noses.

Libby closed her eyes once more for luck.

When she looked again, the fluffy creature standing in the trunk was pretending to be a purple goat balanced on one leg.

Libby giggled.

Unexpectedly, the creature giggled too and forgot to be a goat.

Libby swallowed hard. In front of her stood an enormous purple wolf-like creature.

Libby didn't say anything for the longest while. Was this the Big Bad Wolf? He had the pointy ears Rex had described, but one of them had a red-and-yellow lollipop stuck to the inside fur. He had the yellow teeth and the long claws ... but his breath!

Libby pinched her nose shut.

'Sorry,' said the creature. 'I found a bag of sweets and I was so hungry. Sweet things make me smell.'

'Are you going to eat me? I asked you not to before I opened the trunk but I'm not sure you heard.'

'I don't *want* to,' said the creature, scratching an ear with his left toe. The lollipop flew off and into Libby's bin. Little furry hairs floated up and made her sneeze. 'Would you like me to?'

'No thanks. What would make you smell better?'

His nose dropped to the floor, followed by the rest of his head. It sniffed left and right and landed on her left foot.

Libby felt her insides go squishy like a melted marshmallow. 'You can't eat my foot!'

'That thing. That wearing thing you have.'

She pulled off her sock and held it out. 'It's called a sock.'

The creature took it very gently and stuffed it into his mouth. He sat down inside the trunk and chewed, making all sorts of rolling yummy sounds. 'Am I not scary?' he said between chews. 'I'm meant to be scary. All my family are scary. Everyone I know is scary, really. That's what a wulfen is meant to be.'

Libby frowned. He was beginning to smell exactly as she imagined a caramel sundae might. It was hard to think of something so sweet-smelling being scary, but she looked him up and down properly, just in case. His wolfy paws had long claws but they didn't look as if they would rip her apart. While his snout was like a wolf's, his eyes had beautiful gold and silver flecks in them, like a very small universe of stars.

'You can come out into my room if you'd like.'

The creature nodded. He stepped out onto the red velvet cape and stretched.

Libby walked around him, being very careful not to step on his bushy tail. It looked like a warm rug. She took a deep breath and lifted up his big furry ears to see if he'd washed behind them. 'Do you have a name?'

'Wolfgang Amadeus Rachmaninoff the Third,' he said, in a squeaky voice that was trying to sound BOOMY.

Libby nodded. 'It's a good name.' It was the sort of name to make people *not* trip you up in the playground.

'Most people scream. Especially when I roar.'

He roared, just a little, because he didn't really want to scare her off.

The little roar made her giggle again.

The creature joined in with the giggling.

As he did so, he shrank to the size of a medium-sized puppy, scruffy fluffiness sticking out in every direction. (This was his favourite size, though Libby didn't know it yet.)

She hugged him tightly. 'I'm going to call you Wulfie.'

'I like that,' said Wulfie, and the flecks in his eyes danced.

'Hungry?'

Wulfie's little ears flapped like sails.

'You really aren't the Big Bad Wolf?' Libby asked.

'Oh, wulfens are far more exciting than wolves. We can be tiny as mice or as big as, well, the biggest thing ever. Just like that!'

'You could still eat my brother Rex if you wanted to? He smells like socks. Only I can't imagine he'd taste very nice and you'd have to grow big again because he's a bit bigger than me.'

Wulfie went pale, like the inside of a very hairy purple cucumber, and shook all over so that he tumbled from her hands on to her bed where he bounced himself into a little ball of fluff.

Libby picked him up. He fitted inside one hand.

She patted the part of the furball that she thought must be his head. (It was his bum.) 'That's OK. I wouldn't eat him either,' she said. Wulfie's snout popped out and he licked her hand. 'How did you make yourself so small?'

'Oh, it's easy,' he said, shaking out one paw after the other and whipping out his tail. 'When I'm angry, it's really hard not to grow and it's harder to shrink, but when I'm happy, I can grow big or small just by wanting to!' He stretched bit by bit until he was puppy-sized again and frowned. 'Unless I get scared. Then I go tee-ny-tiny. And if I get wet. That makes me shrink fastest.' Wulfie's tummies – he had three – rumbled like small trains doing loop-the-loops on a rollercoaster and he looked up at her with big eyes. 'Growing and shrinking make me very hungry,' he said.

'Let's go and find some food then. Do you want me to carry you?'

'Yes, please,' he said.

(Wulfie liked being carried. It was his absolutely favourite thing, after smelly socks and just before burping.)

Chapter 6

On the way downstairs, Libby stepped carefully over Malachy, the neighbour's cat, who was pretending to be asleep. She pointed at a door with a big KEEP OUT sign and a picture of a skull and crossbones on it. 'That's my brother's room.'

'Is he dangerous?' said Wulfie.

Libby thought of Rex in a cage and how he'd snarl and rattle the bars. 'Yes,' she said decisively.

She looked in at the bathroom and told Wulfie to never drink from the loo because she'd heard of dogs and cats that did and she didn't know whether wulfens might too.

'Why not?'

She whispered the why into his nearest ear.

'Oh.' He sniffed the loo. It was sparkly clean. 'Smells *clean*,' he said, as if 'clean' was something yucky.

On the next floor down, Libby showed him her parents' bedroom. Then they were in the hall and she pointed out her father's inventing office, full of jars and implements and bits of old things, mostly green. (It was her dad's favourite colour so most of his inventions were green, such as The Wig That Changes Colour and Answers Back, The Umbrella Helicopter That Comes When You Whistle and The Cycle-Spitter That Fires Green Goo at Cars That Get Too Close.)

'Some day he'll be famous but he isn't yet.'

They finally reached the kitchen and the scullery where jars and tins of food were kept.

'We have to be careful not to eat anything that Veronika might notice missing,' said Libby.

Wulfie didn't hear.

His nose was on the floor, sniffing.

It skidded under the cooker, bringing the rest of him up against the cooker door, which flew open and jammed against his bum. When he'd shrunk enough to pull himself clear, Wulfie dragged out a long hard something that might have been a rasher of bacon or a bit of carrot but was so old and covered in mould that it didn't really matter what it was any more.

'Yum!' said Wulfie, gobbling it down.

'Yuck,' said Libby.

They went back to Libby's room with a packet of stale crackers and some shavings of smelly cheese (for him) and a tiny amount of nuts (for her).

Libby spread out a rug and they had a picnic on her bed.

When the food was gone, they sat together thinking stuff and feeling happy and full. Wulfie chewed the tip of his tail while Libby chewed her hair.

'Why were you in the trunk?'

'I was hiding from my brother and my mother and chores,' said Wulfie.

'I never hide,' said Libby. 'They'd only find me.'

Wulfie climbed up on her lap. 'My brother and his friends tease me because I'm the only purple wulfen born in three millennia.'

Libby stroked his ears. 'I'm not sure why my brother teases me. I think it's just for being a girl.'

'I only meant to hide for a bit but then I couldn't open the lid. So I had to hibernate because I was hungry. When I woke up last night and heard voices, I rattled the trunk but the lid didn't open, not until you opened it today, and then I was here.' He went all slumpy and looked suddenly homesick. 'I don't know how to get home again.'

'There, there,' said Libby and offered him her second sock, even though it meant her feet would get cold.

Wulfie cheered up as he chewed. 'My mum's trunk looks exactly like yours, only it can't be the same one because it's there and I'm here. But I *was* there, in it, and now I'm here.'

'It must be a magic trunk – a portal between your world and mine,' said Libby.

She thought for another while and wondered if Zebediah F Flanagan had been a time traveller of sorts, or even part-wulfen, since it was his trunk. If so, did that mean she could be too? Thinking that would be pretty awesome, she checked her ears for fur and ran her tongue along her teeth for sharpness, but they were still stubbornly human.

'Lupuslandia, where I come from, is full of rules and regulations,' Wulfie said. 'When to go to bed and when to get up. How to bow to the King, and what height to carry your tail, and how thick your fur should be, and how you should talk to your elders, and when you can howl and when you can snarl. There are whole Scary Classes where you learn to be a True Wulfen. If you're not exactly like everyone else, they make fun of you. And nobody else is purple.'

'It's a bit like that here,' said Libby. 'The "being different" part, anyway. Veronika, Rex's mum ... she doesn't like me very much, but I don't know why. Dad's nice, just a bit distracted. He's a scientist and an inventor and things like that take up a lot of thinking space. And Rex is my step-brother, to be avoided at all costs.'

Then Libby showed Wulfie her favourite book of maps and her schoolbooks and told him about Granuaile, the pirate queen.

All too soon, the front door banged open. Rex liked to slam doors open and shut. His voice curled around the banisters and trotted up the stairs and under her door. 'Oh, Liiibby. Little Liiibby Louuu! I have the scariest story for you tonight! It's got guts and gore and blood and *everything*!'

Rex's voice worried Libby, but it scared Wulfie so much that when she looked back the wulfen had shrunk to a teapot-sized ball of purple scruffiness – only cuter because he had eyes and ears and a little quivery nose.

'I'll have to hide you inside the trunk.'

'Couldn't I hide in your bed?' said Wulfie. 'I can make myself tinier.' *Ping!* Now he was the size of a mouse.

'Rex always stands on the bed.' Libby put the red velvet cape inside the trunk and placed the teeny-tiny wulfen very gently on top of it. 'You'll be safer here.'

'Don't forget to let me out,' said Wulfie.

Rex had his hand on Libby's door handle when Veronika's voice wrapped itself around him. 'Oh, Rexipoo! Come down this minute! That little runt doesn't deserve any of your great stories tonight.'

'B-but –'

'I'm making hot chocolate!'

Rex stomped downstairs and Libby rushed over to let Wulfie out, terrified he'd have disappeared. She sat him up on the bed beside her and, as he grew back to his favourite size, she told him a story full of smelly socks and chocolate elephants that could fly and parents who loved all their children. There were no bullies in Libby's bedtime story at all, and only kindly monsters.

Finally, when they snuggled into bed for the night, Libby pointed up at the skylight. 'See those stars? My real mother's an explorer so she might be up there. She'll come back soon as she can but you can't rush exploring and she's a very good explorer. '

Libby thought then of Rex and Veronika, of her dad with his experimenting mind. Her home wasn't safe for a wulfen to wander around. Cuddling Wulfie close, she put on her most serious voice. 'Wulfie, you heard Rex. He wouldn't be nice if he found you. And Veronika hates dogs almost as much as she hates mess, so even though you're not a dog –'

'What's a dog?'

'A bit like you but not,' she said, needing to continue before she forgot what she wanted to say. 'My dad's sweet, but he's forgetful and might not remember to keep you a secret even if I ask him to. So I need you to stay in this room and not let anyone see you. Do you understand?'

'Would I scare them too much?'

Looking into Wulfie's eyes, Libby faltered. How could she tell him that people who had never met a wulfen before would find him weird? That they might want to experiment on him to discover why he could talk and change size and eat stinky socks?

'Uh-huh. I think you would.'

Wulfie grinned. 'That's good. I *am* a wulfen and we are *meant* to be scary, but I'm glad you're not scared of me,' he said and licked her nose.

Libby fell asleep curled up beside her new best friend, his tail wrapped around her neck like a comforting scarf.

Chapter 7

Libby bounced out of bed the next morning. It was still dark outside, and damp, but it didn't seem too bad a day, even with all the chores she had to do before school. Not now she had a secret new best friend who was heaps better and scarier than the Big Bad Wolf.

As Libby put on her uniform for school, she worried about what might happen if Rex found Wulfie. 'You can't go exploring without me,' she said, pulling on a pair of black tights with holes in the toes. 'Even if you think the house is empty.'

She tugged up her green tartan skirt and tucked in the cream shirt that was one size too small, before pushing her head and arms through a jumper so scratchy she could feel it through the shirt. 'I'll bring you up some food before I go so you don't get hungry but I need you to promise you won't leave this room without me. Not even if you sniff out the smelliest sock in creation and it's right outside the door.'

Silence.

'Wulfie?'

Libby checked everywhere. He wasn't in or under the bed. Nor was he in the trunk or behind the curtain or in her schoolbag. She even looked in her shoes in case he had become tiny enough to hide there.

Wulfie was nowhere at all.

'Libby!' came Veronika's voice. 'Hurry up with the dirty clothes. We haven't got all day!'

Maybe she had imagined him. Feeling sad, Libby lugged her schoolbag onto her shoulder and hauled the laundry basket downstairs from the landing, one step at a time.

'Coming, Mum.'

Veronika insisted on Libby calling her 'Mum', though she couldn't have acted less like a mother to her. Libby had come to realise that Veronika didn't really like little girls, any more than Rex liked homework.

On the third stair from the top of the second last flight of stairs, a wet tongue appeared from the basket and licked her nose. 'Wulfie!'

Veronika appeared at the kitchen door. 'Are you DAWDLING again? You know what the Big Bad Wolf does to DAWDLERS!'

'He licks the skin off their feet,' said Rex, sticking his head out of the bathroom on the floor above.

'Exactly.'

Libby carried the heavy basket down to the laundry room and unloaded it slowly into the washing machine, knowing that her step-mother would soon bore of watching and leave. 'Remember,' said Veronika, 'you still have to make breakfast and a packed lunch for Rex!'

As soon as the door closed, Libby opened her school-bag. 'You'll have to come to school with me,' she said to Wulfie. 'Shrink and hide inside.'

'Yay! I get to go to school,' said Wulfie with a big grin.

'Sssh.'

He was too excited to shrink. 'You'll have to make me wet.'

Libby quickly poured a cup of water. 'Are you sure?'

Wulfie grabbed the cup from her with his front paws and tipped it over his head. Shrinking to the size of a small pencil case, he jumped into Libby's bag and she did up the straps. It was a very old bag of Dad's and almost falling apart in lots of places.

'What's school?' said a muffled voice.

'*Ssshhh.*'

—

On the way to school Rex hung back to wait for his friends, annoyed that he hadn't been allowed up to scare Libby last night. 'Bet you were scared anyway,' he said as she passed.

Libby felt Wulfie snarl softly in her bag. No matter that he was scared of Rex, it was his wulfen instinct to protect her. Libby lifted her bag off her back and wrapped her arms around it, smothering it with her sleeves. 'Oh no. I mean, yes. I was very scared!' How would she keep Wulfie hidden all day if they couldn't even make it to school?

Delighted, Rex told all his friends. 'She hides under the duvet,' he crowed. 'Sometimes she even wets her bed she's so frightened. Like a baby.'

Libby held her bag in front of her like a shield. Wulfie was growing. She could feel it. She needed to get to school quickly, before he got too big.

'Tell them, Libby. The way I tell a story, you can hear the Big Bad Wolf scraping his claws against the side of that stupid old trunk in your bedroom.'

Libby nodded. He *was* a very good storyteller.

'Complete scaredy-mouse. Even my step-dad says so and he should know.' Rex grabbed Libby's shoulder. 'That trunk is full of dead bodies, by the way.'

But Libby had Wulfie in her bag and, despite his weight and wriggliness, she felt light as air with him there, so she just turned and smiled at Rex.

'Are you listening to me?' Rex pinched her upper arm.

'I might be,' said Libby and ran ahead and through the school gates before he could respond.

Chapter 8

There was a new poster up on the school noticeboard facing the front doors, just as Ms Poddle had promised.

SCHOOL PLAY: ACTORS WANTED
NO EXPERIENCE NECESSARY

All Libby had to do was put her name down. She scuffed her shoes on the linoleum and chewed her lip. Libby wasn't at all sure Veronika would want her being in a play when Rex was the one doing drama lessons. But still ... perhaps it would be OK if she only got a little part?

She was about to reach for the pen that was hanging from the poster when Rex rolled into the corridor. He'd been picking on children even younger than her on the way in and was feeling nasty. Libby didn't know he was there until his hot breath snaked down the back of her neck.

'Seriously?' He laughed loudly and Libby felt herself shrink. She put her hand down to pick up her bag, but Rex stepped on the strap deliberately and called out to his friends. 'Hey, guys, Libby's putting her name down for the play!'

Libby straightened up, feeling a little bit brave. 'I could do,' she said and wondered how Rex didn't notice her bag wriggling.

—

Wulfie had listened to Rex being mean to Libby all the way to school without being able to do anything. He was finding it very hard not to climb out of Libby's bag, grow to full height and swallow the boy whole. Libby had been right – Rex did smell of old socks.

Wulfie didn't like eating boys, despite being wulfen, but he reckoned that if he kept his eyes closed he could maybe pretend he was eating socks. Either way, in Wulfie's estimation, Rex had to go.

For Libby's sake.

But Wulfie couldn't grow in school – he'd promised Libby.

—

Rex wrote his name down in capital letters and held out the pen to Libby. 'Go on, then,' he said. 'Put your name down. Maybe you'll get cast as the stage cleaner-upper.'

Libby didn't move. She was trying to make herself invisible so he'd lose interest and go away.

'Oh wait, maybe you can't write your name yet?' Rex sniggered and his pals joined in as Nazim came down the corridor. 'Want me to write it for you?' Rex said, using his sweetest voice.

Libby decided she liked this less than his mean voice.

'What will it be? Libby the Scaredy Worm? Or Libby Who's Afraid of Everything?' Rex turned to the poster and wrote *Libby the Stinker*.

—

Nazim was just trying to work out how to help Libby when he saw a little purple paw slip out of a rip in the side of Libby's schoolbag.

'Or maybe,' said Rex, pointing at Libby and laughing, 'you could be one of the mice that gets eaten by the

Big Bad Wolf – which will be me, of course.' He was too busy sneering at her to notice the purple paw untying his shoelaces, and then tying his shoes together.

In a triple knot.

Nazim squinted at the poster, then pushed his way into the group. 'Libby,' he said. 'Ms Poddle wants to talk to us about our project before class.' Feeling braver than he normally did on his first week at a new school, Nazim lifted Libby's bag from the floor and walked off, forcing her to follow him down the corridor.

Rex and his pals jeered. 'Yeah, go on, goody-goody nerds.'

'Ooh, careful you're not late ... Might turn into poop!'

Nazim waited for Libby to catch up then handed over her bag. 'Ignore them,' he said. 'Every school has bullies.'

As they turned the corner, chaos broke out behind them and they sneaked a peek. Laces tied together, Rex had toppled, tripped and finally fallen face-first into a bin. Rubbish was everywhere, with Rex in the middle and a piece of toffee wrapper glued to his nose. His

friends were so busy laughing that they couldn't even help him up.

Libby and Nazim looked at each other and raced into class.

—

Their teacher, Ms Poddle, arrived and Nazim took his seat near the window. Rex was last in, a bruise the shape of a squished watermelon already forming under his left eye.

Nazim drew little furry paws peeping out of bags all the way up to break-time. Libby concentrated hard and sneezed whenever Wulfie wriggled, so nobody would notice that she had something alive in her bag. She had to be really careful when she opened it to take out her books in case she pulled out the tickly wet nose of a wulfen instead.

At break-time Libby fled to her safe place under the oak tree. When she was absolutely certain nobody had followed her, especially Rex, she let Wulfie out to have a little climb so he'd tire himself out and sleep for the next few classes.

'You were very good not to grow at all,' she said.

'It's hard to stay small when I want to come out and play.' Wulfie tipped the last of her juice over himself before climbing, stickily, back into her bag.

Back in class, she kept her bag on her lap and pretended not to feel Rex glaring at her. But it's hard to concentrate on maths when you have to cough loudly to disguise the tiny snores coming from inside your bag. She really hoped Wulfie didn't talk in his sleep.

Ms Poddle wanted to know why Libby wouldn't put her bag down. She was on her way over to Libby's desk when Nazim dropped a full pencil case, which exploded across the floor. The teacher was distracted for a moment, and just in time the lunch bell went.

Rex pushed his way out of class. If he couldn't get to Libby – until home time at least – he wanted to use his bruise to scare the little kids in the yard.

Nazim came over to Libby as she packed her books.

'Thanks for helping,' she said.

'I saw him,' he said, as they walked out.

'What?'

'The creature in your bag.' Nazim cleaned his glasses on his shirt and then put them back on to look at her properly. 'Is it a monkey?'

'I've nothing in my bag,' Libby said.

'Oh,' said Nazim. 'OK.'

'See.' She opened her bag. All that was there, apart from her books, was a little purple furball.

Nazim squinted at it, then looked back up at Libby. 'That guy was being really mean to you.'

'That's Rex. He's my step-brother. He's always mean.'

'I'm Nazim. I'm new. Dad moves all the time with work, so I've been to ten different schools so far. Some not so good. Some really weird. You probably shouldn't be friends with me because we'll probably move again in six months.'

'Don't you want a friend?'

Nazim shifted his glasses back up his nose – they were always sliding down. 'More than anything.'

Libby made a decision. Her first brave decision today. 'Promise you won't tell?'

'That we're friends?' said Nazim.

'No.'

'We're *not* friends?' Nazim was puzzled.

'We are,' said Libby. 'Come on. I've got something to show you.'

Chapter 9

Making sure Rex wasn't following them, Libby led the way over to the old oak tree and slipped in behind it.

'This is the coolest place,' said Nazim. 'You can see the whole yard –'

'– but nobody can see you,' Libby finished, grinning. It was a big space, full of dried twigs and earth, hidden by the branches and sheltered from the rain. She hadn't shared it with anyone before. Rex had always driven them away first.

As Nazim watched, Libby lifted the furball from her bag and whispered to it, 'It's OK, Wulfie.'

Out popped a nose.

The nose sniffed Nazim's hand. It tickled and he giggled.

That made two ears emerge, purple and quivery. Then paws, then a fine fluffy tail.

Nazim grinned. 'It's, like, the smallest, most perfect wolf in the world!'

Wulfie stepped from Libby's hand into Nazim's. 'Why thank you,' he said, holding out a paw, 'but I'm a wulfen, actually. We're far scarier than wolves.'

'And it *talks*!'

'He,' said Libby. 'Wulfie, meet Nazim. Nazim, this is Wolfgang Amadeus Rachmaninoff the Third. Also known as Wulfie.'

Wulfie grew a few more inches. (He liked to have a long snout when being introduced. He thought it made him look distinguished. It was a wulfen thing.)

Nazim blinked and pushed his glasses up his nose with his free hand. 'Can he grow to any size?'

'I can,' said Wulfie. 'It's a skill of mine.'

'I wish I could,' said Nazim.

'Me too,' said Libby. 'But he says he can't always help it – that when he's angry, it's really hard not to grow even if I've asked him to stay hidden. That's why,' she said, producing a bottle of tap water from her bag, 'I keep this nearby. Wetting him is the only way to make him instantly small.' Wulfie moved onto her lap as she unwrapped her egg sandwich. 'But shrinking and growing makes him *really* hungry.'

Nazim opened his lunchbox. 'Would he like some halva?'

'Is it sweet?'

Nazim nodded.

'Better not,' said Libby, giving Wulfie some of her sandwich. 'If Wulfie eats something sweet, you do *not* want to be in the same room afterwards. He was really smelly when I found him because he'd been eating lollipops.' The egg sandwich was gone and Wulfie was beginning to smell like melted jellies. 'So far his favourite food is a smelly sock.'

'Gross,' said Nazim.

'Yeah, but when he eats stinky things, he smells unbelievably sweet, like strawberry jam and meringue and toffee and hugs.' She stopped, thinking she'd said too much, but Nazim grinned.

'Which is awesome! My mum would love him,' he said. 'Dad does marathons and his socks are seriously stenchy. She's always trying to get him to throw them out. If we had a Wulfie, she could just get him to eat them!'

—

Before they went back into class, Libby decided to cross her name off the list on the noticeboard. Nazim went with her. 'Don't you want to be in the play?' he asked.

'Rex would be horrible if I got a part. It's not worth it.'

'Course it is. He's horrible already.'

Libby giggled. 'He really is.'

'You can always say he put your name down, which he did, sort of. You're just changing "the stinker" to your surname. Correcting it, like.'

'I'm not sure he'd see it like that,' said Libby and made her second brave decision that day. She crossed out *Libby the Stinker* and wrote her name clearly at the end of the list: *Libby Lou Flanagan*. 'It's not as if I'd get a bigger part than him anyway,' she said. 'Rex goes to drama classes outside school.'

'Put my name down too,' said a muffled voice in her pocket. 'W-O-L-F-G-A–'

'I can't, Wulfie.'

'I know I'm a wulfen, but my great-great-great-great-uncle was a wolf. At least that's what Dad says when he's mad at Mum, which is often.' Wulfie sounded sad, thinking about home.

Libby put her hand into her bag and stroked the little wulfen between his ears. Even when your family was mean to you, she knew you could still miss home.

'You would be an awesome wolf,' said Nazim, adding his own name to the list.

Libby stroked his tiny nose (Wulfie's, not Nazim's). 'You really would. You'd be the best and baddest wolf *ever*, but I have to keep you a secret, remember?'

'Because I'd scare people?'

'That's right.'

—

After school, Nazim walked home with Libby as far as Sasuke's house. She introduced dog to boy and stayed there stroking the dog as Nazim walked off up the hill, the Spire in the distance with a neat little cloud on top shaped like a pig.

Wulfie's nose popped out of her bag, sniffing right and left. 'Food!'

'No, Wulfie. Remember you asked me what a dog was? Well, Sasuke is a dog and dogs are friends, not food.'

Sasuke barked in agreement.

Wulfie barked back. He was ready to play.

'Wulfie, *shh*.'

Sasuke licked Wulfie's nose. Wulfie blew air into the dog's ear and Sasuke howled. Wulfie's ears danced.

'Sasuke, stop. Wulfie, keep out of sight and *stop* growing!'

Because he was. It was the friendliness of the dog and the happiness of having friends. Wulfie's whole head and one paw were sticking out of her bag.

Libby spotted Rex coming around the corner.

'Please, Wulfie, shrink before he sees you!' She sounded scared, which made Wulfie frightened and he shrank just in time.

Rex walloped the back of Libby's head so hard she stumbled and nearly fell. 'Come on, sis. Happy families!'

As they drew nearer to home, Rex linked arms with her and put on his best Big Brother Face – just as Veronika opened the door.

'Such a darling boy,' she said, kissing the top of his head.

'Yuck,' said Rex, but his mother thought this was cute.

'Isn't he the best big brother a girl could have?'

'Oh, sure,' said Libby.

'Do I smell cheekiness?' said Veronika.

Then she noticed the bruise.

Chapter 10

Veronika turned Rex's face to the light and howled. A tiny howl, but still. 'My poor darling boy! Tell me now, who could have hurt my Rexipoo? Your poor face!'

Libby was heading quickly upstairs to start her homework before she was given any chores to do, but she still heard exactly what Rex said next: 'It was Libby. Libby pushed me over.'

His mother shrieked. Her shriek filled the hallway and bounced up the stairs to snag Libby's ankles. 'Libby Lou, you come down here THIS INSTANT!'

Libby retraced her steps. Slowly.

'I knew you had nastiness in you! Did you punch your brother?'

'He fell over,' said Libby. 'I didn't do anything!'

'She tied my laces together,' wailed Rex.

'I wasn't anywhere near you!'

'Well, if *you* didn't tie his shoelaces together,' said Veronika, 'who did? Why would my darling boy lie about such a thing?'

Libby could think of lots of reasons, mostly to do with Rex being mean, but she could feel Wulfie's paws pushing against the side of her bag and it was all she could do to keep him hidden. He was desperate to get out and defend her, maybe even to gobble up Veronika.

'You're going to tell me it was an invisible gnome?' said Veronika.

'Oh, yeah,' said Rex. 'Maybe it was the Big Bad Wolf!'

'Rex, that's enough,' said Veronika. 'You smell like a rubbish truck. Go wash up. Libby, I'll deal with you later because I can't think of anything bad enough to punish you, short of getting the Big Bad Wolf to come and nibble a finger or two. I'm sure I'll have thought of a punishment by tomorrow, but I don't want to hear from you until then.'

Libby traipsed upstairs, feeling hungry and unloved. She unpacked her books and opened her homework journal, trying not to think of anything much at all.

She sighed three times, but quietly, and pulled on her mother's jumper for warmth.

Wulfie tried to cheer her up by bouncing on the bed and falling down. Twice.

It didn't work.

So he tried shrinking and talking in a tiny voice, but Libby was concentrating hard on deciding whether to do the most difficult homework first or to start with something she liked.

When he couldn't even get her to smile, Wulfie wrapped his tail around her like a fluffy coat, but Libby unwound it gently and placed him back on the bed.

'Wulfie, I know you wanted to help me by tying Rex's shoelaces together to get back at him for being mean, but Rex is *always* mean. Tomorrow you have to stay at home.'

Libby started her maths homework, trying not to feel hungry or sad.

Wulfie pulled the red cape from the trunk and wrapped it around her shoulders to keep her warm. She stroked his ears and lifted him up onto her lap.

'You don't know it yet but it never ends well with Rex.'

—

Dad came up after dinner and emptied two roast potatoes from the pocket of his favourite green jacket. The jacket had silver buttons, each with a different scientific symbol, and he thought it quite dashing. When she'd heard him coming, Libby had asked Wulfie to hide under the bed. He was curled up there inside one of Libby's old jumpers being very quiet because he really, really wanted to make her happy again.

'Dad, I didn't push Rex. He's miles bigger than me!'

'Is he, Mouse? Is he really?' Dad liked to talk in questions. It made him feel more like a grown-up. He was the quiet sort of scientist with dust under his fingernails and a moustache with leftover breakfast bits. He was happiest when alone with numbers and parts of things and whirry bits.

'Yes. He is.'

'Do you think that really matters in the grand scheme of things?' He took off his glasses and cleaned them with his tie. There were spaceships on the tie.

'What things?'

'That's my girl. Keep asking questions. It will make your brain so much more resilient. Lovely velvet cape, by the way, though it would be nicer in green.'

And then he was gone, leaving Libby befuddled and no wiser.

'It's not fair,' she said.

Wulfie crept out from under the bed and hugged her as much as he could. He didn't like meanness or injustice or hunger. Libby suffered from all three, and hugs were the only thing he seemed to be able to do that didn't make her feel worse.

—

The next day, Libby got up early and did her morning chores. She was hoping Veronika might forget to be mad at her if everything was spick and span. Then she did her evening chores too. She polished the hall floor and the landing, washed all the windows and the sinks and the bath and peeled potatoes for the evening meal.

The auditions were going to be directly after school, so if she had all her evening chores done *before* school, maybe nobody would notice if she was late home. Besides, Veronika would most likely be watching Rex at the audition. If Libby auditioned right at the end, Veronika wouldn't even know she was there.

Finally, Libby picked a flower from the back garden to put on the tray with her step-mother's breakfast.

'What do you think you're doing?' snarled Veronika.

Libby froze.

'She wants to audition for the school play,' said Rex. 'That's why she's being extra nice, with the flowers and stuff. It's funny, really.'

Veronika laughed. She had a sharp laugh, like cut glass. 'How ridiculous!'

Rex moaned and clutched his face. He whispered in his mother's ear. She was plucking the flower, one petal at a time, with her sharp nails.

'That's my clever boy! Rex has suggested that as the first stage of your punishment for knocking your poor brother into a bin and damaging his good looks, you are grounded tonight. You will not stay late at school and you will not audition. I'm doing you a favour, really. It would be a complete waste of everyone's time. You can walk home alone and your father will let you in.'

She crushed the flower and ate her breakfast, chewing each mouthful twenty-five times because she had read somewhere that it would keep her young.

'If he remembers,' she added.

Chapter 11

Libby walked home alone from school, her steps heavy and slow. Everyone, including Nazim, was staying on for the auditions. She stopped to stroke Sasuke as she passed and the dog looked at her sadly, as if he understood how she felt. Then she walked the rest of the way home, trying to think happy thoughts about flying pigs and bottomless ice-cream sundaes and how good it was that it wasn't raining.

Her dad did remember to let her in. He gave her a very absent-minded hug that smelled of walnuts before rushing back to his lab to experiment with doorknobs that would electrocute people you didn't like and car alarms that would shriek and cling to thieves.

Libby ran upstairs to see Wulfie. It had been a long day, with Rex talking over and over about the auditions and how he was going to show everyone what he could do, and she really needed a hug.

'Wulfie?'

But Wulfie wasn't in her bedroom.

She opened the skylight in case he was out on the roof.

She looked in the laundry basket, the washing machine and Rex's smelly sports bag. Then she hung up the washing and cleaned the kitchen, hoping Wulfie would have appeared by the time she went back upstairs.

'Wulfie?'

The room was cold. Libby shut the skylight, but then put on the red cape over her mother's jumper and opened it a smidge, so he could sneak in even if she was asleep. Worrying about Wulfie wouldn't bring him home, so she decided to work on her poster for the play. She still had several little wolves to colour in.

Ms Poddle loved her design but had still made Libby stop and take up her book for reading time yesterday *and* today, when Libby wasn't *nearly* finished. There was so much more in her head than she could put down.

CRRRASH!

The door flew open and Libby jumped, giving one of her wolves a very, very long tail.

'Ms Emily said the bruise made me look fiercer,' said Rex. 'Do you want to see my impression of the Big Bad Wolf?'

Before she could nod, Rex jumped up on her bed, fluffed up his messy hair into two pointy ear shapes and roared.

'That's really scary,' said Libby. 'You'll be a great wolf.' She wanted Rex to leave. Vanish. In a puff of smoke ideally. Leave her to feel sad about Wulfie being lost.

Surprised at this, Rex grinned and plonked himself down on her bed. 'You know, I will be. It's the only role I've ever wanted. I get to scare EVERYONE!'

'Brilliant.'

Libby meant it. Maybe he'd stop scaring her if he was scaring everyone else.

'Mum took me for a caramel-and-chocolate sundae. I was so full, I couldn't finish it.'

Libby had never even had a scrap of leftover sundae. She couldn't help sighing. It was only a tiny sigh, but the sadness in it seemed to make Rex feel happy.

'It was the best one yet,' he said and bounced out the door without trying to scare her once.

He left footprints on her duvet.

Wulfie would have licked the duvet clean, Libby thought and dusted them off as best she could. She didn't feel like drawing any more and curled up under her duvet, counting spots of mould on her wall, thinking sadly of all the worst sorts of things that could have happened to Wulfie.

He might have fallen down a drain, been kidnapped by a zoo-keeper or taken in by a family who put a collar on him or locked him in a room and made him play dolls or sold him to scientists for experimenting on.

Libby was so busy worrying that she didn't hear the trying-to-be-quiet thumps over the nearby rooftops, and she jumped when a *thunk* hit the skylight. A purple fluffy *thunk*, followed by a very bouncy Wulfie tumbling in.

'Where have you been?' she said, relief running through her. 'Did anyone see you?'

'The school and lots of people.' He was grinning from ear to purple ear. 'I auditioned!'

Libby blinked. He couldn't have – could he? She swallowed before saying, very slowly: 'Wulfie – you know you can't be in the play.'

'Because I can't let anyone see me?'

'Right.'

He looked sad for a moment and Libby stroked behind his ears. 'Were you pretending?' she asked.

Wulfie shook his head, looking as serious as he could. 'I didn't let anyone see me. I kept myself in the shadows all through the auditions, and I only talked to the director when she left the hall to go home and no one else was around. I think you're right about me scaring people, because when she saw me, she just rushed to her car ...'

'Oh, Wulfie, no!'

Wulfie was reliving the moment. 'Only I said *hello* very politely and asked if I could audition and then I did the wolf thing.' Up and down her little room, Wulfie showed Libby how he'd done the Stalking Walk, the Prowl, the Roar (but silently) and the Flexing of the Claws. Finally, he puffed up so much that his puffiness filled the room.

Libby began to sneeze because the room was so full of purple hair.

'Can you –' *sneeze* '– please –' *sneeEEEZE* '– shrink a bit?'

When Wulfie was back to puppy size and Libby had stopped sneezing, he jumped up on her lap. 'The director said I was a natural. I was fierce and I was kind, gentle yet savage underneath. She loved my costume! That must be another name for skin or fur, I think,' he said. 'I wanted to see what it would be like, and since you couldn't go, but you really, *really* wanted a part ...'

Libby had a bad feeling about this. 'Wulfie, who did you say you were?'

Wulfie grinned. He felt clever all over. 'I said I was Libby Lou Flanagan the First.'

Chapter 12

Nazim was waiting for Libby at the school gate. 'You got the lead role!' he said with a grin.

Libby hurried to the noticeboard. Rex was still a block away, dawdling. He and his friends had been trying to think of nicknames for their teachers, all of which used the words 'poo' or 'pee'.

She looked at the list of names posted up on a big white sheet of paper under the title of the play. There they were in black and white. The names of those who had got roles. Nazim was Main Wall, House Made of Hay, and Rex was Pig Number Three – but Libby was the Big Bad Wolf.

She felt the hairs stand up on her neck.

'This'll be fun,' said Nazim. 'You must have been awesome! Everyone knows baddies are the most fun to play.'

'It's a long story,' said Libby, frowning.

'What's wrong? This is wicked!'

'I didn't audition,' she said in a quiet voice. 'I was grounded.'

'Then how –?' Nazim frowned and his glasses slid down his nose. 'Who –?'

Libby nodded at her school bag.

'Oh,' said Nazim.

Libby couldn't see a way out. 'I would have been happy to be a tree. Rex wouldn't mind me being a tree.'

Nazim spun around. 'Speaking of Rex ...'

Libby's brother was coming down the corridor with his mates. Libby took off at speed with Nazim following. As they turned the corner, they heard Rex roar: 'You have GOT to be kidding me!'

—

Libby could feel Rex glaring at her all morning. Ms Poddle called her up in front of the whole class to congratulate her. Rex glared even more and sharpened pencils to fire at her from his desk.

When the bell went for break-time, Rex waited for Libby in the corridor, so she stayed behind and asked Ms Poddle about her play. 'I see the wolf as the last romantic, waiting to be converted to vegetarianism and never eating meat again,' said Ms Poddle. 'I must say, I am surprised you got the part. You always seem so ... *dreamy*.'

Up to lunchtime, Libby's class worked on their posters. Rex's arm had a very steady aim. His pencils hit her several times. When the lunch bell went, Libby dived out of class. Seeing Rex pack up quickly to follow, Nazim dropped his bag. Several books spilled out and blocked the doorway so Libby could get away.

The two friends met behind the oak tree.

'What do I do?' Libby bit into an apple, ignoring the bruises from when Rex had bounced the apple off the counter before she packed their lunches.

'You could try to explain to the director that you have a small purple wolf –' said Nazim.

'*Wulfen*,' said a small voice from her backpack.

'Ssh,' said Libby.

'And that he auditioned for you.'

'*I'm not small.*'

'He really isn't, normally,' said Libby. She opened her bag and let Wulfie out. He was the size of her pencil case if it had been round and furry. 'He's also meant to be at home in my room.'

'It's boring being alone,' said Wulfie. What he really meant was that he hated leaving Libby on her own and unprotected, but if he said that, she'd only worry more, and he was trying to be good.

Libby reached into her bag for her lunch. Half her egg sandwich was gone. 'Wulfie, if you have to eat half of my food, can you please not leave slobber on the rest?'

Nazim offered her half of his tikka masala samosa. 'Mum thinks any leftover food works in a samosa. You should try it. It's really good!'

But Libby had lost her appetite.

'I'll have to let Rex have the part,' she said, giving Wulfie the rest of her sandwich. 'It's the only thing to do.'

—

All the cast gathered in the school hall after lunch to meet the director. Rex was waiting for Libby and he tripped her up as she went in.

'You'll get into so much trouble now, sneaking out of the house. Wait till I tell Mum!'

Everyone who had got a part gathered on the stage behind the curtains. Even the trees and shrubs, the Smog Monster and the narrating mouse. All of them were missing class. It was like a party in a secret room. Everyone was excited – except for Rex, who was scowling.

Libby kept as far away from her step-brother as possible.

The principal arrived and clapped her hands twice to quieten them down. She introduced them to the director, who waited for them to sit in a circle before she spoke: 'My name is Ms Emily Farminier, but you may call me The Director.'

Libby gasped. It was Rex's drama teacher!

Rex sat up straight.

'As you may know,' Ms Emily continued, 'I am a very, VERY famous director, but I also used to attend this school. I have decided to gift this school my expertise for this particular play because I am EXTREMELY fond of wolves.' She flicked her long hair from side to side. It had a long white streak, like a badger, and seemed to move all by itself. 'This play is not only going to pay for a new enclosure for them in the zoo, where they can romp and roar.' She leant forward, as if seeing each and every one of them. 'It will also make the world sit up and worry about their plight for years to come. It may even get them to realise that, in the end, wolves are the superior species.'

Ms Emily clicked her fingers and the principal handed out copies of the script to pass around.

She clicked her fingers again and the principal disappeared.

It would have been far more effective if the principal had actually vanished or a trapdoor had opened under her feet, but she just tiptoed backwards instead, almost bowing to the director's back. *How very strange*, thought Libby.

'Get to know your parts. Tomorrow we do a read-through at lunchtime.'

Libby jumped up before she lost her nerve. 'He can have it,' she said, pointing at Rex. 'The Big Bad Wolf part. I don't even want to be the wolf and he really does.'

'Nonsense,' said Ms Emily. 'You were magnificent!' She turned to the assembled students. 'Wait till I tell you about this girl. She finds me, in the car park, when I am

going home. I'm tired. It's been a long few hours. Some children talented, lots,' she sniffed, 'not. She finds me there. In her costume. And she says, "I want to be the Big Bad Wolf. I can be the best wolf you ever saw."'

That doesn't sound like me, thought Libby, chewing on her hair while watching her toes.

Ms Emily sighed. 'Of course, I said no. Auditions were over and that was that. But then!' She flicked her hair back and forth until it looked like waves on a stormy sea. 'She roars – and what a roar it is. The hair stood up on the back of my neck and applauded. Such wolfiness. Such power ... and the most magnificent costume! You, Libby Lou Flanagan, *are* the talent in this show,' she said.

Libby looked up. Everyone was smiling at her.

Except Rex. He was scowling through a mouthful of sweets.

But he wasn't saying anything. Mean or otherwise. *Maybe he doesn't want Ms Emily to know what he is really like?* thought Libby.

Before the children went back to class, Ms Emily handed out a schedule. 'Every afternoon and weekend we will have rehearsals. You will have to be at every rehearsal for your scenes. We have four weeks to be magnificent!'

—

Rex was waiting for Libby by the school gate, blocking her route out of the yard when she left with Nazim.

'Oh, look,' said Nazim, pointing at the sky. 'An albatross!'

Rex looked up. He wasn't even sure why. Libby dodged past and Nazim caught up with her. 'I think I'll walk home the long way today, past your house,' he said.

Rex's friends punched Rex on the shoulder for making them wait for his sister. As a gang, they ran past Libby and Nazim and headed on, making up for wasted time.

Libby and Nazim walked slowly, keeping their distance from her brother. 'He can't do anything,' said Nazim. 'You heard the director.'

'You don't have to live in the same house as him. It's not as if he can only pick on me at school.'

Nazim took an old sock out of his bag. 'I found this at home.' Wulfie's snout appeared out of the corner of Libby's bag. 'It's one of Dad's marathon socks – I thought Wulfie might like it.'

'I'm not sure he deserves a treat,' she said, but she gave it to him anyway.

'Sorry,' said Wulfie through a mouthful of sock.

Libby loosened the flap of the bag to give Wulfie more chewing space. 'I really don't know,' she said to Nazim, 'how to be a wolf.'

As Libby's bag began to smell like sunsets and ice-cream, they stopped to stroke Sasuke. Libby was in no hurry to arrive home. The dog tried to lick Wulfie's nose and Wulfie growled – he was busy eating his favourite food of all. Libby told him to behave.

That was when Nazim figured it all out.

'He'll just have to teach you,' said Nazim, pushing his glasses up his nose and grinning like a lemur. He had one crooked tooth, like a trainee fang, that made him look both mischievous and wise. 'Wulfie will have to teach you how to be a wolf.'

Chapter 13

Veronika was pacing the carpet in the sitting room. Back and forth, up and down. The carpet would have crawled into a corner if it could have to avoid her heavy feet.

'I don't see how Libby could have got any part at all,' she said and stopped to glare at her husband. 'Unless she sneaked out of the house and hid until we'd left the auditions?'

'I was with her all evening.' Libby's dad crossed his fingers behind his back.

'Spoiling her, no doubt.'

'Doing maths.' He really wanted to scratch his moustache but kept his fingers locked. 'She's quite good at maths.'

'Jack, dearest, Libby isn't good at anything. She's *your* daughter!'

'Oh,' said Dad, 'of course,' and he scratched his chin.

The clock ticked and chimed the hour. Then it ticked some more. Still Veronika paced up and down. Libby's dad felt dizzy and hid behind a newspaper.

'I've got it!' Veronika froze like a tub of ice-cream. 'I know exactly what happened. The director got Libby's name mixed up with Rex's.'

—

Veronika stormed up to the school in her stompiest boots. She found Ms Emily in an office, working out a timetable for rehearsals. Veronika told Ms Emily that, with the greatest respect, she must be mistaken.

The director said she was certainly not mistaken. 'I am a person who is never mistaken. Being mistaken is something that happens to other people who are far less clever than me, and I do *not* like anyone suggesting I could ever be mistaken about anything!'

Veronika was having trouble following everything Ms Emily said, so the director made it very clear: 'Your daughter was the most magnificent wolf I have ever seen.'

Veronika laughed, assuming this was a joke.

'You should be very proud,' said Ms Emily.

'Of *her*? Oh.' Veronika frowned. 'You're serious.'

'I'm *always* serious,' said the director, and showed her the door.

—

The whole cast were meeting that morning in the library for a read-through of the script. Libby made Wulfie a nest at the back of her locker and told him to stay there. 'It's only till lunchtime,' she said. 'Then I'll take you behind the tree and let you climb or teach me wolfy stuff.'

Wulfie licked her nose. He turned three times, wrapped his tail over his snout and settled down for a long nap.

Rex was right behind her when she closed the locker. 'Talking to yourself, sis?' Libby jumped, and he went off laughing to himself.

—

'Let's read the script from beginning to end,' said Ms Emily, 'and acquaint ourselves with the story.'

Libby read her lines, quietly at first. They all did. But as the scenes passed, she grew braver and her voice grew louder. She understood the wolf. He was an outsider. He was lonely. He was always hungry.

Ms Poddle's script was a cautionary tale. So, unlike Rex's Big Bad Wolf, when Libby reached the last scene with Pig Number Three, her Big Bad Wolf decided to spare the pig and become vegetarian instead. And everyone cheered. Then Rex spoilt it all by asking, 'Great joke, but where's the real ending where the wolf rips the pig apart?'

'The pig played by you?' said Ms Emily.

He went quiet then.

—

Libby gave her step-mother a picture she'd drawn of Wulfie. 'That's the costume the director wants me to wear in the play.'

'As if I'd make a costume for you!' said Veronika.

'Ms Emily said it had to be magnificent and you've been making such wonderful costumes for Rex, year after year. She says nobody else would be able ...'

Veronika liked to be complimented. 'Oh, well, if she

said that, I might give it a go. But Rex's costume will take priority.'

Libby held out the bag of purple fur she'd collected from her room and her pockets and her schoolbag and her locker and her duvet. 'She said to give you this, as a sample. You can cover the costume with it. There'll be more in a day or so.'

'A purple wolf, how ridiculous.' She squinted at Libby. 'Where are you getting this fur *from*?'

'School,' said Libby, crossing her fingers behind her back. It wasn't *exactly* a lie. Wulfie shed fur everywhere.

—

As Head Coach of Wolfing, Wulfie took his role seriously. Knowing Libby needed his help saved him from feeling just a little bit homesick from time to time.

'Key wulfen moves to master,' he said, 'are the Stalking Walk, the Shleeving, Spook-Tiptoe, Slithering and Loping-Like-Evil-Snake-in-Heels.'

He laid down the velvet cape on Libby's bedroom floor to muffle their feet and showed her each of the walks, one by one.

But all they did was make Libby laugh.

'They're *scary*,' said Wulfie.

'No,' she snorted, curling up and holding her tummy because it hurt so much from laughing, 'they're really not!'

Wulfie sat in a heap on a roll of his tail and looked so sad that Libby threw her arms around him. 'Maybe it's only because I love you so much.' She gave him a great big cuddle to make him feel better and said a small white lie. 'I bet they'd be scary for Nazim.'

Wulfie agreed.

'Maybe I should learn my lines before you teach me to be a wolf?'

Libby had a lot of lines to learn, but she was used to remembering stuff. She'd learnt her twelve times tables while hoovering the stairs and her periodic table cleaning the toilet and the bath and the sinks.

Rex, on the other hand, was having problems memorising his lines. He only had five, but Libby could hear him getting them wrong, over and over again, in his bedroom. And in the kitchen. And in the sitting room.

'Oh, for goodness' sake!' she heard Veronika, who rarely lost patience with Rex, say. 'Even that little runt upstairs can learn her lines!'

'I'm not a runt,' said Libby to herself. 'I'm nearly as tall as Rex.'

She and Wulfie were dragging a chair across to block the door in case Rex came up for revenge, when Veronika's voice beat them to it.

'Libby Lou Flanagan, get down here and clean this sink properly!'

Chapter 14

Libby suddenly had even more jobs to do around the house. On top of rehearsals and homework and watching Rex lie around doing nothing at all. It was exhausting. She felt like one of those mice running around in a treadmill, juggling eggs and polishing shoes and doing all sorts of pointless things.

It did seem pointless, housework. As soon as she'd cleaned one room, Rex made sure it got dirty again. He spilt things that he didn't need to spill, rubbed mud off his shoes onto every rug and left dirty dishes upside-down all over the place.

'Libby will soon make a botch of being the Big Bad Wolf because she's so tired,' Veronika said to Rex.

'Then,' she went on, making sure Libby was listening, 'you, my genius son, can be the biggest, baddest wolf.'

Wulfie, who hated meanness, growled from the confines of Libby's trouser pocket. She had to yawn loudly to cover up the sound.

'Are we boring you?' said Veronika. She was sewing the arms onto Libby's costume – extra long, because she was fully expecting Rex to get the role in the end – and had bits of purple fur all over her clothes.

Libby shook her head and fastened her hand around the pocket to stop Wulfie wriggling out.

'It was made for me, that part.' Rex's voice cracked, just a little and he tipped the crumbs from his plate onto the floor.

Veronika poked a finger at Libby. 'Clean that up,' she said.

'He'll only spill more,' said Libby.

'Don't be petty! Rexipoo isn't petty, are you, dear? Not even when his greedy little sister steals his part.'

Any minute now, Wulfie was going to burst out of her pocket. Libby turned away while she swept the crumbs into the dustpan.

'What's in your pocket?' said Rex.

'Nothing.'

Rex walked towards her, frowning. Libby backed away.

'You're hiding something!'

'Toilet wipes!' Libby whipped a packet from her other pocket. 'Got to go. Loos won't clean themselves,' she said and disappeared.

—

Every school lunchtime, Wulfie, Nazim and Libby met under the oak tree. Wulfie continued Libby's wolf lessons, with Nazim doing lookout. On Wednesday, it was raining so the yard was empty, but they went out anyway. Since they didn't have to worry about being overheard, Wulfie decided to teach Libby 'the three sounds that every wolf must make: the Howl, the Roar and the Snarl'.

The Howl was easy. The Roar, not so much.

'Maybe you don't need a loud roar?' said Nazim. 'Rex isn't very loud, but everyone's afraid of him. Think about Rex and the stories he tells you.'

Libby did and this time her roar was deep and very scary.

Nazim grinned. 'Awesome!'

As for the Snarl, Libby couldn't do it. Her mouth wasn't made to curl up and her vocal chords weren't used to making mean sounds.

—

Tiredness from all the extra chores caught up with Libby towards the end of the first week of rehearsals. Ms Emily was explaining to some of the actors how they could *pretend* to be House Number One with pieces of cardboard that would be covered with straw when Libby fell asleep backstage.

Her snores brought the entire cast to investigate.

Ms Emily sent a note home on official school paper asking for Libby to be excused from chores, just as she was excused from homework until after the opening night.

But Rex was watching his sister closely. He saw her rushing to her locker and he had seen the way she cradled her bag in class. He even saw her putting food into her pocket and noticed that she'd become extra good at not running into him alone.

At lunchtime on Friday, Libby hung back until everyone had left the classroom to avoid bumping into him. But just as she was about to open her locker to take Wulfie out, Rex cornered her. 'Go on,' he said. 'Open your locker.'

'Me? No,' Libby dropped her locker key into her bag and looked around for some way to escape.

'Open it up,' said Rex, sneering. 'Or I'll pick the lock.'

Just then there was a shriek from the girls' loos and several students flew past. 'It's haunted. The paper dispenser is HAUNTED!'

In the confusion, Libby dived past Rex and into the girls' toilet block. Wulfie was inside the toilet roll dispenser, running faster and faster. The cubicle was filling with paper, accompanied by Wulfie's happy sniggers.

'Out. Now!'

Wulfie plopped into her pocket as the toilet roll ran out. 'That was fun!'

—

If she couldn't stop him sneaking out of her locker, Libby decided Wulfie would have to stay at home. 'You can coach me in the evening and I can concentrate on rehearsals without worrying about where you are or if you're going to get caught.'

Wulfie agreed, but looked as sad as a cake left out in the rain. It was like being back home in Lupuslandia when nobody wanted to play with him because he was purple or too messy or not scary enough.

Since Libby didn't want him to be sad, she had left him picturebooks to look at and snacks to eat and left the skylight open so he could sit on the roof. But she still found him hidden at the bottom of her coat pocket the next day when she put her hand in to get her locker key.

He bit her finger because she'd poked him in the nose.

The following day Libby found Wulfie curled up in her lunchbox having licked the crumbs from the corners. It was empty because Veronika disliked letting Libby off her household chores, which had included making Rex's lunch, and so made herself feel better by not giving Libby any lunch at all.

On the third day, Wulfie hid in Libby's ear, the size of a fly. She only noticed when he started snoring. She had to ask to go to the loo in the middle of maths so she could pull him out by the tiniest of tails and slip him in her pocket without anyone seeing.

Libby was learning that it is very hard to stop a wulfen from doing naughty things. She could hardly raise her voice or shout, because nobody was meant to know that wulfens existed, let alone that a purple one was hiding in her pocket.

Since Wulfie came to school even when she asked him not to, Libby decided to keep him in her bag and bring her bag to rehearsals. But it was hard to rehearse when she also had to keep a tight hold of her bag to make sure a tiny wulfen wasn't sneaking out of it.

'Hey, sis,' Rex said on the Wednesday, 'why don't I look after your bag?' He smiled at Ms Emily. 'So she can act.'

'Thank you, Rex,' said Ms Emily, 'but I'd like you and the other pigs to go into the auditorium and practise looking for truffles in mud. Libby can leave the bag under her chair.'

Rex stomped off.

'Don't forget to practise oinking, all of you. And remember, you don't have hands and noses – you have trotters and snouts!'

—

Nazim shared his lunch with Libby each day, but when she nearly fainted at rehearsal, Ms Emily sent another note home saying that Libby needed double lunches for the duration of rehearsals, to include several biscuits – 'Wolves need biscuits, chocolate is best' – and a piece of fruit.

Libby hinted that the director might reduce Rex's lines if she thought Libby wasn't being fed. She also asked for egg sandwiches, not because she liked them but because they were the smelliest food she knew.

And if Wulfie was well fed, he was much better at sleeping.

Chapter 15

During the second week of rehearsals, rumours spread that a hole had suddenly appeared in the ceiling of the principal's office. As if something huge had fallen through. It had left a pawprint on the principal's blotter. A big pawprint.

As soon as the lunch bell went, Libby ran to her locker to see if Wulfie was safely inside.

All she found were balls of Wulfie's fur.

'He'll be hiding somewhere,' said Nazim. 'Come on.'

While everyone was talking about a giant rodent and saying the school would have to call in an exterminator to track it down and kill it, Libby and Nazim whizzed around the school looking for her wulfen friend.

First they checked Libby's coat pockets and her sports bag. Then they looked in the sports lockers and made up an excuse to visit Lost Property. While Libby checked the girls' toilets, Nazim checked the boys'. Then they split up and looked inside and behind all the bins in the school, trying not to be spotted by Rex or anyone else.

They had just checked under the oak tree when the bell went to call them all back to class. Libby and Nazim trailed across the yard, not knowing where to check next. They were at the back door to the school when Libby heard a 'Psst!' and a tiny 'Oi!'

Hidden behind a potted fern, Libby could just make out a tiny purple snout and two bright eyes. She put her bag down beside the pot and pretended to be tying her shoelace so the mouse-sized Wulfie could climb inside without anyone noticing.

'Gotcha!'

Rex.

'You HAVE got something in your bag,' he said triumphantly.

'No, I don't. All I have is school books and lunch and –'

Rex stepped on Libby's foot without warning, and when she jumped, he snatched her bag. 'You are going to get into so much trouble if this is a puppy,' he sneered, unfastening the straps. 'Mum'll probably boil it or something. You know how much she hates dogs. They'll probably throw you out of school and then I'll *definitely* get your part in the play.'

While Rex was busy glaring at her – his eyes did look a little *piggish*, she thought – Wulfie slipped out unseen.

'Please,' said Libby. 'Give it back.'

'You heard her.' Nazim was standing behind Rex trying to look fierce. 'Give her back her bag.'

'Or what?' Rex tipped Libby's bag out onto the ground. Books and pencils and pens spilled everywhere. No puppy. No Wulfie.

As Rex turned away, disappointed, Libby saw her little wulfen friend perched on her brother's back. His tail was growing, which meant the rest of him was too. Quick as anything, she threw her bottle of water over Rex's back, drenching him and plucking the now-tiny-as-a-snail Wulfie off before Rex could turn around.

Then she fled.

'Wait till Mum hears about this,' Rex roared, dripping with water.

—

Libby didn't speak to Wulfie until they were safely inside one of the toilet cubicles and then she was very cross. 'I told you to stay out of sight!'

'I got hiccups.' He looked very ashamed.

He explained that he *had* meant to stay in the locker, but somewhere on the way to lunchtime, without even really thinking about it, he had made himself small as a penny and accidentally slid through a vent in the locker into the school's air-conditioning system.

'I met some mice. Little Lily May, she is the coolest mouse *ever*. She has blue paws from the time she landed in an ink pot. We played chase all through the air tunnels, only I got hiccups. I held my breath for ages and ages, but then I hiccupped a really enormous hiccup and I just grew huge and fell through the ceiling into that room.'

Luckily the office had been empty.

'I got an ouchy.' Wulfie held out his paw for Libby to remove a splinter.

Libby did it as gently as she could and kissed his paw better. Back to his favourite size of medium-sized puppy, Wulfie snuggled in for a hug.

—

'It's no use,' Libby said when she was walking home with Nazim. 'How can I concentrate on acting when I don't know where Wulfie is going to be or what he's going to do?' They stopped to stroke Sasuke and she lowered her voice so as not to wake Wulfie. 'What if Rex catches him?'

The dog licked her nose as thanks. He hadn't had many pats that day on account of it being cold and everyone else being in a hurry to get home.

'I'll have to drop out of the play,' said Libby. 'It was a stupid idea anyway.'

'Don't give up yet,' said Nazim. 'Meet me here before school on Monday. I think I have the solution.'

—

Unable to punish Libby for the water-dousing, in case the director took it out on Rex, Veronika told her son to avoid Libby at all costs. 'That will make her suffer,' she said.

Since it had become clear to Veronika that Libby was not going to fluff her part, Veronika decided that Pig Number Three was by far *the* most important role in the play: 'The hero who saves the day!'

Because he loved his daughter, Libby's dad was making purple paws for her costume, with retractable claws, and her own ear-swiveller, but this was a secret. Libby hugged her dad tightly when Veronika wasn't looking.

'Doesn't Ms Emily say that the best way to play a role is to *become* the role?' said Libby one evening. 'Maybe we should call Rex *Piggy* for the duration?'

'Nonsense,' said Veronika, frowning. 'It merely means that no pork will be eaten in this house while my darling is playing a pig.'

—

On Monday, Nazim was already at Sasuke's house when Libby arrived, stroking the dog while he waited.

(Veronika was dropping Rex to school each day so he wouldn't tire himself out before rehearsal. This made it easy for Libby to leave home early and unseen.)

'Allow me to introduce the bribe-to-behave sock,' Nazim said, removing a plastic pouch from his pocket.

Wulfie's nose appeared through a hole in Libby's bag. It sniffed left and right. 'Sock!'

'Wulfie, if we give you this sock –' Libby began, and then turned to her friend. 'Is it stenchy?'

'*Seriously* stenchy,' said Nazim.

'Wulfie, Nazim will give you this seriously stinky sock to eat during rehearsals but ONLY if you stay in my bag and don't get seen by anyone.'

Wulfie nodded. He dreamt about the sock all morning until Nazim took it out of the pouch just before they went into rehearsals. A tiny paw ever so gently lifted it out of Nazim's hands and then all they heard from Libby's bag were small sighs of happiness.

—

For days, the socks worked like a dream.

Wulfie stayed quietly in Libby's bag until lunchtime, dreaming of the socks to come. While they rehearsed, he sat in her bag and munched his way through sock after sock. The beautiful smell that came from her bag day after day made everyone feel happier than anything.

'Has your dad not noticed they're missing?' Libby asked Nazim.

'I only take one, but when he can't find the pair, since they're all either lefts or rights, he throws the other one out so I can take that too. Meanwhile, Dad buys a new pair and Mum's delighted. Win-win.'

—

Libby stood in front of the mirror in the school toilets. The tiles were cracked but she liked them that way. They looked like a giant tree, branching upwards. She drew her lips back and practised a snarl. It didn't seem scary to her so she did it again and again. She tried thinking of Rex and how mean he was.

It made her angrier and angrier that her snarl was not scary, until finally she snarled so deeply and full-throatedly that she made herself jump.

'Nailed it,' she said, grinning.

Chapter 16

'I'll huff and I'll puff and I'll blow your house down!'

Wulfie wasn't happy with Libby's lines.

'Wolves don't speak like that! Well, OK, I had a great uncle Rufus who spoke like that, but still, he was *mean*. He'd give the warning *after* he'd eaten the pigs, while burping. So where are the pigs? Will it be, like, a feast?'

'The pigs are Mary, Yoshi and Rex,' said Libby. 'It's a play. Nobody gets eaten. It isn't real.'

'Then what's the point?'

'It's fun pretending to be someone else.'

'Oh.' He scratched behind his ear, thoughtfully. A cloud of purple fur lifted into the air and settled on the floor around him. 'Like when I try to be a furball so no one will know I'm a wulfen?'

'Sort of.'

'A real wolf,' he said, 'a really scary wolf, would never sound so mean. Nobody was scared of Great Uncle Rufus because they were already gobbled up.'

'You're right,' said Libby. 'Rex never says he's mean and that makes him scarier.'

When Libby mentioned this to the director, she was waiting for Ms Emily to say, 'How many wolves have you heard speak?' but she didn't. 'The Big Bad Wolf doesn't have to *say* mean things,' said Libby. 'He probably doesn't think he's mean at all. Most mean people don't.'

Ms Emily thrust her shoulders back as if they were angel's wings and stared into space. Then she smiled at Libby and said, 'Marvellous. I love it. What do you suggest?'

'Well, maybe, instead of saying, "I'm bigger than you and stronger than you", because it's sort of obvious that he is, he might say, "But don't you understand that a wolf has to eat too? It's not that I *want* to eat you – but you are pigs and that means you're food"?'

'Perfect.'

—

'So this,' said Wulfie, 'is the most important move of all, which is why I kept it until last.'

They were in Libby's bedroom. It was a Saturday morning and sun was filling the room, apart from the cat-shaped shadow thrown by Malachy the neighbour's cat. He was snoozing on top of the skylight and dreaming of slow-moving mice.

Rehearsals didn't start until lunchtime, so Veronika had taken Rex out for a nice brunch to give him energy for his first rehearsal of the pigs' dance number.

'It's called the Frightening Fearsome move,' said Wulfie.

To demonstrate, he drew himself up to his fullest height, hit his head on the skylight and fired Malachy upwards and into a nest on a nearby tree.

'Now you do it,' said Wulfie.

'I can't,' said Libby.

'You just have to think yourself big.'

'Humans grow a little at a time until we're twenty-one,' said Libby. 'We can't just change size on demand.'

Wulfie deflated into a wulfen the size of a litre of milk on the end of her bed. 'How can you scare people if you stay small for so long?'

'I don't scare people,' Libby said, plonking herself down beside him. 'Rex does.'

—

With a week to go, Nazim ran out of socks.

'Dad's replaced every set of socks he owns. He thinks Mum's been throwing them out so he's keeping his kit in the boot of the car.' With a little grimace, he produced a smelly sweat-band he'd found at school, but it wasn't the same.

While the cast were trying on costumes prior to rehearsal, Wulfie slipped out of Libby's bag. He didn't stay out for long, just enough to eat a box of very sweet cupcakes that Ms Emily had left sitting backstage.

So, even though he did sit quietly in Libby's pocket when the cast lined up for their warm-up exercises, even though he did stay tiny as a mouse and even though he didn't wriggle or sniff or anything, Wulfie began to smell *awful*.

When it came to the bouncing warm-up exercise, Libby held her pocket shut so he wouldn't fall out.

'Libby, are you OK?' The director came over. 'You look slightly green.' She made the mistake of coming a little too close to Libby's pocket. 'My goodness, what *is* that terrible smell?'

(The trouble is that something as sweet as cupcakes, icing and all, make a wulfen smell not just awful, but stenchy, hold-your-nose-and-run-screaming-from-the-room awful. And with all the bouncing, Wulfie had also thrown up in Libby's pocket.)

When Ms Emily fainted, Libby lifted her hand off her pocket and the stench was released.

The school was shut down immediately and everyone was sent home.

—

Libby walked home slowly that evening. She didn't even stop to stroke Sasuke or mind too much when Rex barrelled past and knocked her into a puddle.

'I stayed quiet,' said Wulfie. 'I didn't speak.'

'But you stole food and now the school is closed and the play might not even happen. Oh, Wulfie,' she said, 'can't you just behave for once?'

—

Back in her room, Libby almost missed her chores. The play would go on. A call had come through confirming that the school had been checked and cleared. They would rehearse through lunchtime tomorrow to catch up. She ran through her lines and tried to get excited about the play, but all she felt was tired.

'Libby?' asked Wulfie.

'I'm busy, Wulfie.'

'It's OK.'

Libby tried to carry on, but Wulfie was very quiet. Too quiet. He was never *that* quiet. She spun round, half-expecting him to have sneaked out, but there he was on her bed, small and fluffy, sucking the end of his tail. In front of him was her science book, open at the dissection of a frog.

'Why do people do this?' he said.

'Scientists do it to see how creatures are inside so they can make them better and cure diseases and stuff. It's only done after they're dead.'

'Was this frog dead?'

She nodded.

Wulfie chewed his ear. 'I have three stomachs. I can grow and shrink and you can't. Would the scientists want to know what I was like inside?'

Libby sat down on the bed and lifted him onto her

lap. 'Wulfie, nobody is going to find you and I wouldn't let anyone hurt you, not ever.'

'Not ever and a hundred days?'

'Not ever and a hundred thousand days.'

'Is this why I can't be seen, for real?'

She nodded.

———

For the rest of rehearsals, Wulfie was very careful not to be seen and not to fall through ceilings. In the privacy of Libby's bedroom, he helped her with her lines, and when they practised under the tree during break-time, he gave her feedback on her walk and her snarls and the wolfy menace in her voice.

By the end of the day of the dress rehearsal, Libby was stalking the stage as if she had a tail and a backbone covered in fur. She flexed her fingers as if they had claws, wriggled wolfy muscles in her shoulders and yawned as if she had sharp teeth.

'The Big Bad Wolf is here,' said the director.

Chapter 17

The audience was filing into the hall, buzzing and chatting. All the cast were in the classroom nearest the stage getting into make-up and costume and bouncing with excitement. Veronika positioned herself in the middle of the front row so Rex would see her smiling at him.

Libby was so excited she could hardly breathe.

Leaving her head, paws and feet in the classroom, she went and sat in the 'haunted' toilet cubicle that nobody else would use. Looking in the cracked bicycle mirror her father had given her, she snarled, to the left and to the right, and wriggled her body in a fluid wolfy way.

Wulfie was hiding in her sleeve, itching to get out and into the loo-roll dispenser again, when the door was kicked open.

It was Rex. All pink and piggy.

'Enjoy your moment, dung beetle.'

Rex meant to sound nasty, but since he'd forgotten to take off his piggy snout, it just sounded weird instead. He lifted up his snout and scratched his nose.

'Tonight is your worst nightmare. You're going to get on stage and everyone will laugh because no way are you a wolf! You're a scared mousey dung beetle and if they don't laugh at you because you're rubbish, I'll make you look extra rubbish so they *do*. The play will be ruined and everyone will blame you!'

Satisfied, he turned to leave.

Libby jumped up and ran after him. 'Don't,' she said.

'*What* did you say?'

'Please don't spoil it, Rex. It's not fair on everyone else.' Rex barely moved. 'It's fun, isn't it, doing this play? And it's for a good cause.'

'You think I care?'

Libby was desperate. 'I bet nobody will mention the wolf tonight. They'll all be talking about what a great pig you were!'

Some of the girls who were acting the parts of mice came in to check their make-up and Rex sauntered out. Libby couldn't see his face, but she knew he was grinning.

She could still swap costumes with Rex and stop him ruining everything. She knew all his lines. She knew everyone's lines. He'd be happy and nobody would know until ...

But they would.

Rex was not very good, even at playing his own part. He'd ham it up and ruin it anyway. And maybe he wouldn't *really* do anything at all. Maybe he'd just been trying to scare her?

After all, that was what he did.

—

Back in the classroom, everyone was dressed and ready to go. Ms Emily rolled in, her hair pulled up into a long tail that reminded Libby of Wulfie's. The director made eye contact with each and every one of them. 'You know what to do. This is your night to shine. Be thrilling and break a paw!'

She chortled at her little joke. The cast were all too scared and excited to say anything.

'A little stage fright is normal. The important thing is that you enjoy yourself, girls and boys. Now, places backstage for Scene One and Scene Two please!'

Libby put on her wolf's head and threaded the cord for the ear-swiveller down her sleeve so she could control the movement of her long furry ears. It was a big head – Libby was actually looking out through its mouth, past rows of yellow teeth.

Ms Emily whispered into one of Libby's wolfy ears, 'Be spectacular.'

To Rex, she said, 'Try not to fluff too many of your lines.'

—

Libby padded backstage in her wolfy feet and into the wings. She let Wulfie slide down her sleeve into a corner behind some empty boxes while everyone in Scene One, including Nazim, got into position on stage. 'If you stay here, you can see it all, but *please* don't let ANYONE see you.'

Wulfie nodded and licked her nose. Nazim gave her a thumbs-up from the stage. He was ready with his cardboard props to be the best Wall Made of Hay ever seen on stage. Libby wasn't on until the end of the scene, and although she knew she should feel nervous, all she felt was excitement.

—

Wulfie *meant* to be good.

It wasn't as if he *wanted* to be bad.

But Rex had threatened to make his best friend in the whole world look stupid.

Very quietly, Wulfie crept forward. Keeping in the shadows, he sat on a coil of rope near the curtains where he could see Libby at all times and rescue her if need be.

The lights went down on the audience. All you could hear were whispers and breathing on the dimly lit stage, until the music began that would set the scene of a world where pigs spoke and made houses from straw.

The curtains went up, taking all the rope with them. Wulfie, whose tail was caught in the coil of rope he'd been sitting on, was swept up above the stage into the rafters.

Rubbing his bruised tail, he settled down on a rafter to watch the show.

He could *definitely* see everything now.

—

Libby slipped her paws on to test her yellow retractable claws and discovered Rex had filled the fingers with itching powder. There wasn't time to do anything so she channelled the itchiness of it into her performance. She became a ratty, scary wolf who waved his arms around a lot.

The itching had worn off before she was due back on stage to terrorise Pig Number

Two. Since her costume was very hot, she took a deep drink of water before slipping her head back on.

Too late, she realised that Rex had filled her flask with chilli flakes.

But Libby would not let her brother ruin the play. Not for anything. She turned her wheezes and coughs into snarls and mini-howls.

By the time Rex came on stage as Pig Number Three, he had been tripping everyone up backstage and telling them they were stupid and useless and all sorts of nasty stuff. He built his brick house, but by now, the children who were holding up his cardboard 'brick' walls and all the nearby trees were trembling with fear of him. Everything seemed to be shaking a little on stage, as if there was a breeze blowing.

After weeks of trying to behave and being nice to Libby all through rehearsals, Rex had finally snapped. Ms Emily hadn't taken the part of the Big Bad Wolf from Libby and given it to him, so now he would show his drama teacher what a mistake she had made. He would be the best and scariest pig, far scarier than the Big Bad Wolf.

You see, Rex knew he was a genius. His mother kept telling him so.

So when he came on stage, Rex didn't bother with his lines, not even when Ms Emily began prompting him from the wings. Instead he talked about pigs and how clever they were. He looked at his watch. 'Ooh. I guess it's time for the Big Bad Wolf to come. I'm SO scared. Like, *p-p-petrified.*'

The audience was laughing.

Libby hesitated. Rex was right. She wasn't scary at all!

Then she spotted Wulfie's tail dangling down over the rafters. How had he got up there? His tail was growing longer with every word Rex said. That meant

Wulfie was getting angrier. Even if he didn't pounce and gobble Rex up, Wulfie would soon be so big that he'd fall and squish him. Libby had to stop Rex or Wulfie would reveal himself to hundreds of people.

More afraid of losing Wulfie than she was of Rex, Libby roared from the wings. A real roar that froze Rex to the spot centre-stage. It didn't sound human. It sounded *wolf*-like.

The Big Bad Wolf sloped onto the stage, eyes fixed on Pig Number Three. She flexed her claws. *Snap*.

'Remember me?' said the Big Bad Wolf, pointing a sharp claw. 'You've spoken about me often enough. About my yellow teeth and my long claws. I must say I'm flattered.'

Libby stalked across the stage and snarled at Rex.

'Of course, I ate your brother and your sister. I ate lots of tasty little pigs, and now ... And now ...'

One of the braver little trees tripped Rex up as he backed away. He landed on his cardboard axe and cowered. The Big Bad Wolf lowered wolfy jaws over the pig and the audience – who had completely forgotten that this was a girl in a wolf costume and not a fearsome beast – gasped.

Then, to the surprise of everyone, the Big Bad Wolf sat down beside the pig, lifted the pig's head gently onto her lap and howled. She howled with all her might, as if she would never be scared of Rex ever again.

And Libby, the biggest baddest Big Bad Wolf, spoke. 'Your fear has changed me. The way you cowered made me realise I no longer want people to be afraid of me and I no longer want to be a bad-tempered bully. That taste of power, the glory in their terror, is gone. From now on,' she sighed, 'I shall be a vegetarian wolf.'

Chapter 18

The curtain came down.

Silence.

Rex tried not to scream. He was suddenly afraid of the dark, seeing monsters everywhere.

Libby held her breath and her wolfy nose. She had scared Rex. All by herself!

Wulfie slid down the curtain in the dark. He scurried across Rex's feet – Rex shrieked, but it was a very quiet shriek – and leapt up into Libby's arms for a nose nuzzle. She took off a paw to let him slip up her sleeve seconds before the curtains opened and the lights came on.

Then they heard the applause. Hundreds of hands clapping and mouths shouting 'Bravo!'

Libby couldn't stop grinning. Wulfie felt snugly warm and tickly all at once, like a wriggly arm-muffler.

The cast held hands and bowed. Even Rex.

Ms Emily came on stage, removed Libby's mask and led her out in front of everyone. They all bowed again and again.

—

None of the audience was allowed into the classroom until the cast had changed. They gathered in the corridor outside, proud and sometimes surprised parents and siblings, smiling aunts and uncles and happy wolf-lovers; an excited murmur of voices that erupted into words of congratulations as soon as the cast began to file back out.

'Out of this world!' said Ms Poddle to the children. 'They will be talking about this show for decades to come. As for the wolves! The wolves in Dublin Zoo will have the best enclosure of any zoo in the world!'

'There she is!' The principal shook Libby's hand. 'Amazing. As for your costume – most unusual, a purple wolf!'

'I made it,' said Veronika. She found herself ruffling the girl's hair. (It was actually quite nice hair, she decided.)

Libby wasn't sure she liked having her hair ruffled, though it was a novelty that Veronika was being nice to her. Wulfie was in the pocket of her coat so she ruffled his hair to see if he liked it. He bit her finger – playfully – in response.

Everyone made way for Ms Emily, who smiled and complimented everyone, including the students who had been trees and bales of hay. She stopped in front of Rex. 'For the first time in all the years that you have been coming to my class, Rex, tonight I saw you actually act. Congratulations! But, Libby, yours was the most powerful performance I have seen on stage since my own acting days. How did you learn to roar like that?'

'Oh, y'know. Practice.'

Veronika was frowning.

Libby hatched a plan. She smiled up at Veronika and crossed her fingers behind her back. '*Mum* taught me,' she said, pointing at Veronika. 'She used to be an actress herself.'

'How impressive.' Ms Emily flicked her fringe with a long red fingernail and turned to Veronika. 'You must send Libby along to my class.'

'Maybe we could celebrate with a caramel sundae,' said Libby in front of everyone and before she lost her nerve.

'What a good idea,' said Veronika. She was still in shock. 'Who'd have thought it,' she said. 'Little Libby Lou.'

Chapter 19

Rex waved his pink pig's nose in Libby's face, swishing it back and forth like a broom and forcing her backwards until she bumped into the trunk in the corner of her room. 'I don't know how you did it, but NOBODY upstages *me* in the scary stakes.'

He jumped on to the bed, bouncing Wulfie – who was doing his very best impression of a cuddly toy of great adorableness – onto the floor behind him. 'It's OK, though. I have a really yucky story for you tonight.' He scratched a pimple on his nose. 'Well, more a creature than a story, but enough to give you nightmares for weeks and weeks.' He landed at Libby's feet. 'You might even wet your bed and catch pneumonia and then your teeth will fall out and I'll make them into a necklace and do voodoo with them.'

Libby wished he would go away. She'd had her first ice-cream sundae and had been feeling happy and full before Rex came in.

'He's called the Shadow Soul Snatcher and he's far worse than Mum's crummy wolf. When he moves, you can hear the screams from his tummy of all the girls he's eaten.' Rex was proud of this bit. It had that nice extra bit of scariness that would last into the dark when he left his sister alone.

Behind Rex, Libby saw Wulfie straighten his ears and wriggle his claws, but she didn't say a word.

Not even when he started to grow.

Not even when he licked his lips.

Not even when he was two feet taller than Rex and looked as if he wouldn't mind at all being asked to eat this horrible smelly boy.

Because most people would mind.

A lot.

First, Rex was smelly. He hadn't changed his lucky underpants since rehearsals began four weeks ago. Second, he thought firing himself into muddy puddles or jumping off walls into steaming piles of dog poo was fun. Third, he loved picking his nose – and eating what he found there!

Unaware of the huge wulfen standing behind him, Rex continued his story. 'So there's this enormously hairy spider. A spider with fangs the size of elephant tusks, dripping with blood. The girl doesn't know where to go and backs into the corner. Only the corner is where the Shadow Soul Snatcher lives in the big smelly trunk. They're friends, see. The spider and the Snatcher.'

Rex lifted Libby's arm and wiped his nose on her sleeve.

(As he did this, he noticed that Libby wasn't crying.

She wasn't even shaking.

Or begging him to stop.

Oh well. He'd have to be nastier.

Much nastier.)

He raised his arms, fingers spread into claws, so that his shadow grew up along the wall behind Libby. 'The Snatcher leans down over the face of the terrified little girl, an icy veil of goosebumps dangling like a spider web above her head.' Rex lowered his voice to a demonic whisper: 'Then he opens his mouth and the smell is like screaming inside her skull.'

Libby knew she should warn Rex. But, for some reason, she smiled instead.

A big toothy grin from ear to ear.

Because there, right behind Rex, looking over his nasty little back, was Wulfie.

And Libby said nothing.

She didn't say *Watch out* or *Look behind you* or anything at all.

Nada.

Zilch.

Not even when Wulfie's big purple jaws and long sharp teeth were open over Rex's head. Instead, she giggled.

Rex looked furious. 'You should be in tears by now.' A dribble of drool landed on his head.

'Wulfie, no,' Libby said quietly. 'Don't.'

Rex looked up just in time to see the inside of Wulfie's big purple mouth closing over his little red head.

'*Aaggghhh!*'

Rex hung onto Wulfie's big front teeth. 'HELP!' he shouted. And then he was gone. Sucked up into Wulfie's

mouth. All of him. Head – *suck* – hands – *suck* – feet – *double smelly suckaroonie.*

Wulfie closed his mouth with a great big happy slurp.

As Libby saw the tip of her brother's second boot disappear between Wulfie's long teeth, she gave a little shudder.

She picked up Rex's piggy nose, which was all that remained of her brother.

Quite a big part of what Libby was feeling was extreme happiness. Even though she knew it was wrong. Well, it had to be: Wulfie was eating her brother. No little girl is meant to enjoy watching her brother being eaten. But then no little girl, she hoped, had such a nasty brother.

'Oh, Wulfie,' said Libby. 'You are bold.'

Wulfie grinned. 'Do you really think so?' he said in his best posh accent and gave a tiny burp that smelled of boy.

'Oh, yes!' said Libby. 'You really are.'

Chapter 20

The thing you need to know about Wulfie's insides is that they are more enormous and more smelly than anything we have as humans. We have one stomach. It potters along and pretty much digests everything.

Wulfie has three.

He also has a throat full of nooks and crannies that are home to all sorts of dislikeable creatures, such as the Stinky Sugustingbugs who live off slime and crawly things normally found in cowpats and dung. They have twenty legs each, covered with tiny toothy prickles, and are incredibly good at weaving their favourite foods out of leftovers.

None of these creatures was happy to see all the slime they had collected flushed down Wulfie's throat as Rex slid past. To slow his descent, he tried to hold on to some Stinky Sugustingbugs, but it didn't help.

They bite. Like mosquitos.

He slid into the first stomach. It was like a hot bath – Rex's least favourite thing, after Libby. It is there to clean the food.

The next one is the slime stomach where food gets coated in a nice green goo that softens the food.

—

'Spit him out.'

Wulfie looked down at his toes and hummed a tune.

Libby stepped right up to him. 'Wulfie!'

Wulfie put on his most innocent look. Eyes wide open, ears tucked back ... As if he hadn't just swallowed the smelliest little boy in the whole world.

Libby stamped her foot on the floor, trying to look fierce. 'You have to spit him out. *Now.*'

'But –' said Wulfie.

'Please.'

'But he's so mean. Every little bit of him is mean.'

'You can't eat my brother.'

'Why not?' asked Wulfie.

Libby had to think about that. Life would be so much easier without Rex around. For a start, he wouldn't do nasty things on purpose so that she would be blamed. He wouldn't tell her scary stories that kept her awake all night. Her step-mother might be nicer to her without him around.

She sighed. 'If Rex disappears ...'

'Yeah?'

'They'll only blame me,' Libby said.

—

Rex was hanging over Wulfie's third and deepest stomach. He had flexed his legs against the walls so he wouldn't slide in, but was losing his grip. The green goo he was drenched in made him slippery, while the whooshing around part of being swallowed had made his legs wobbly.

Every drop of sweat that dripped off his nose spat fireworks that lit up the pit below in all its awfulness. Little creatures called Spitglossums were circling, waiting to play with his bones. They were reddish-blue with the thinnest of fingers and very hungry. Their job was to digest everything and reduce it to mush.

Rex was scared.

So scared, he hadn't thought of how he would wreak revenge on Libby when he got out.

Just as he lost his footing, Wulfie burped.

It was a whale of a burp that spun Rex backwards, followed by a roar of complaint from all the hungry little Spitglossums.

Up he spun, bum-first, through the other stomachs, up Wulfie's throat, past his long, sharp teeth and onto the floor at Libby's feet.

Chapter 21

Quick as a small snake in a field of snake-biting-ants, Libby flung a large glass of water over Wulfie to make him shrink. She would DEFINITELY be in trouble if Rex told Veronika she was keeping a giant purple boy-eating wulfen in her bedroom.

Rex's eyes were tightly closed.

He didn't see Wulfie's ears pop down to tiger size.

As Wulfie's nose shrank to the size of that of a baby sloth, Rex's eyelids fluttered, but by the time he opened his eyes, Wulfie was the size of a small purple mouse.

Except for his tail.

The water had missed his tail and it was still the length of a small lion's.

Veronika came stomping up the last few stairs as Wulfie crawled very quietly under Libby's bed. He wasn't able to make his tail shrink because he was feeling boy-sick, which is very like seasick and very like carsick but worse than both.

'If you say anything to your mum,' Libby warned Rex, 'he'll eat you again and I won't say stop.'

Rex wondered who she was talking about.

Thump. Thump. Thump. (Veronika had heavy feet.)

Wulfie tugged his enormous tail in under the bed just as Veronika charged in, all prickly heels and a nose like a small bitter orange.

She looked at Libby standing by the bed.

She looked down at Rex, who was sitting on the floor staring at his feet.

'Rex was telling me a bedtime story,' said Libby. She turned to Rex and smiled sweetly. Libby knew how to smile sweetly. It normally got her into trouble, but right now, she didn't care. 'Isn't that right?'

Rex stood up. He wiped one slimy green sleeve across his mouth and opened his mouth to speak. A tiny gob of something slimy and green slithered out. It fled up the wall and out through a gap in the skylight. (It was probably a Stinky Sugustingbug. They hate light almost as much as they love slime.)

'I won't have you spoiling your sister like this. She might think she's important.'

It didn't take long, thought Libby, for Veronika to forget to be nice to her. At least she'd had an ice-cream sundae now.

—

As Veronika fussed Rex out of the room, Libby climbed into bed and pulled her duvet up to her chin. It was a thin duvet, but she pretended it was full of goose feathers and duck down and maybe even magic fluff that would make the sound of lullabies as it heated up.

Wulfie crept out from under the bed and shook himself dry. This was a bit like watching a furry car go through a car wash. The shake at the snout moved into his ears then worked its way along his back and into his tail.

Thinking he was dry because his nose and ears were, Wulfie jumped up onto Libby's bed. His bum, which was still shaking off the water, shook him back off the bed onto the floor. Libby reached out and picked him up.

Back in bed, he snuggled into the crook of her arm, with only his nose poking out above the covers. 'You were an awesome wolf,' he said. 'Almost wulfen.'

'You taught me how.'

She fished out a plastic bag from under her pillow. Inside was Wulfie's 'ice-cream sundae': a smelly vest she'd sneaked out of Rex's sports bag earlier. She gave it to Wulfie and he howled, very quietly, in delight.

'We're a team,' said Wulfie, burying his nose in the stench of the vest. 'You and me – together we're three.'

'No. We're two.'

'But three rhymes better.'

'Fair enough.'

—

That night, for some reason he didn't understand, Rex had to crawl in a circle three times on his bed before he could fall asleep. He felt entirely discombobulated, as if he'd been turned inside out, bounced about and put through a smoothie maker before being put back together again. His ears were even a little pointy and furry, but not so you'd notice and only until morning. That's the thing about being swallowed by a wulfen – you don't feel quite *yourself* for quite a while.

Of course, by then, Rex decided he must have dreamt it all, though for a few days afterwards he avoided Libby's bedroom, without really knowing why.

—

In her room upstairs, Libby fell asleep looking up at the stars, feeling warmer and happier than she ever remembered feeling up until that day, with Wulfie burping quietly beside her, smelling as sweet as cinnamon toast with honey and maple syrup and chocolate chips.

We hope you have enjoyed reading *Stage Fright*,
the first book in the Wulfie series by Lindsay J Sedgwick.
You can ask your local bookshop about other books
in the series.

The following few pages will introduce you to some
other books by Little Island, which you might
also like to read.

www.littleisland.ie

CHOP-CHOP, MAD CAP!

By Juliette Saumande
Illustrated by Sadie Cramer

Meet Madgie M. Cappock, also known as Mad Cap, of the Rent-a-Hero agency – no job too big or small.

Madgie and her partner in crime Norbert Soup follow a series of clues to solve a mystery involving a missing butcher, an evil cat and weird old Mrs Mudrick across the road, who seems to have it in for them. On top of all this, Madgie's mum's been acting really strangely and – wait, why is Norbert wearing a giant yellow bunny suit?

Can the young superheroes figure out what's going on before it's too late?

'**A really fun, light-hearted, wacky read.**'
Sunday Independent

littleisland.ie/books/chop-chop

THE FREE RANGE DETECTIVE AGENCY

By Jed Lynch
Illustrated by Stephen Stone

Seamus the private
detective is no chicken.
He's a turkey.

Seamus runs the Free Range
Detective Agency. He might
not be the best detective in
town. In fact, he could be
the worst. But he's the only
one who is also a turkey. And, with a little help from his
friends, he usually, somehow, cracks the case.

Each book in the Free Range Detective Agency series
contains a postcard you can use to write to Seamus.
And he'll write back!

'I laughed so much I laid an egg. GENIUS.'
Dustin the Turkey

littleisland.ie/free-range

BUMPFIZZLE THE BEST ON PLANET EARTH

By Patricia Forde
Illustrated by Elina Braslina

Bumpfizzle is an alien sent to Earth on a mysterious mission from Planet Plonk. Or is he a ten-year-old boy who is jealous of all the attention his parents are giving to The Baby?

'So hilarious! Patricia Forde is definitely the high queen of Irish comedy.'
Eoin Colfer, author of *Artemis Fowl*

'The book was funny. It was very funny. I'd recommend it to my friend Brooke. You don't know her.'
Sienna (age 11) for the *Dublin Inquirer*

WINNER OF A WHITE RAVEN AWARD FROM THE INTERNATIONAL YOUTH LIBRARY

littleisland.ie/books/bumpfizzle

HOW BILLY BROWN SAVED THE QUEEN

By Alison Healy

Illustrated by Fintan Taite

What do you do when the Queen is struggling with a knotty maths problem that only you, Billy Brown, can explain? You travel to her palace in the middle of the night and help the nation, of course! In return, the Queen now wants to come and visit – and you can't say no to royalty.

But the Queen's suitcase contains two tiaras, a spare crown, three evening gowns, a silk dress and a pair of green wellingtons – nothing remotely suitable for visiting the bottle bank. Fitting in is tricky when you're so magnificently different.

> **'Clever, quirky and oodles of queenly fun –
> suffering ducks, one was most amused!'**
> **Alan Nolan, author and illustrator**

littleisland.ie/books/billy-brown

Acknowledgements

Wulfie lurched into my life, looking for snuggles and smelly socks, many years ago. Because my daughter and I loved him instantly, I began looking for a way to share him with the world.

I'm writing this in a time of social isolation that has turned the world upside down, even more than finding a wulfen in an old trunk in your bedroom would, so I'd love to thank all those who believed in him as much as I did and held their hearts open.

Huge hugs go to my first readers: Asiya Crandall, Lucia Connolly Yanes, Tanvir Bush, Nazim Choudhury, Dee Barragry, Gary Hetzler, Mary Esther Judy and Jude Fay. I'd also like to send a massive whoop and swirl of joy and gratitude to Siobhán Parkinson who loved

Wulfie from the start and all at Little Island who got us to this point.

Finally, for my daughter Libby, without whom I might never have created Wulfie, I offer thanks for listening, and contributing to Wulfie's early mutterings and mischief. For being there with me through the highs and lows of this journey.

Lindsay J Sedgwick, June 2020

ABOUT LITTLE ISLAND

Little Island Books publishes good books for young minds, from toddlers to teens. In 2019 Little Island won a Small Press of the Year award at the British Book Awards. As well as publishing a lot of new Irish writers and illustrators, Little Island publishes books in translation from around the world.

www.littleisland.ie

RECENT AWARDS WON BY LITTLE ISLAND BOOKS

The Deepest Breath by Meg Grehan

Winner: The Judges' Special Prize,
KPMG Children's Books Ireland Awards 2020

Shortlisted: The Waterstones Children's Book Prize 2020

Mucking About by John Chambers

Selected for the IBBY Honours List 2020

123 Ireland by Aoife Dooley

Winner: Children's Book of the Year (Junior),
An Post Irish Book Awards 2019

Bank by Emma Quigley

Winner: The Literacy Association of Ireland
Children's Book Award 2019

Dangerous Games by James Butler

Winner: The Great Reads Award 2019

Dr Hibernica Finch's Compelling Compendium of Irish Animals by Aga Grandowicz and Rob Maguire

Winner: Honour Award for Illustration,
Children's Books Ireland Awards 2019

ABOUT LINDSAY J SEDGWICK

Lindsay is an award-winning screenwriter and creator of Punky, the first mainstream animation series worldwide in which the central character has special needs (Down's syndrome). It is available in over a hundred countries. She has written for film and TV, games and apps, and the stage. Lindsay started writing about Wulfie in a shed with a pet snail called Percival (adopted from her daughter) and finished it in the company of a scruffilufagus dog called Roxy, who has the heart of a wulfen.

www.lindsayjsedgwick.com

ABOUT JOSEPHINE WOLFF

Josephine is an up-and-coming illustrator and communication designer from Berlin represented by Lemonade Illustration Agency. Josephine likes illustrating characters for animated films, creating fantastic worlds for children's books and finding the right story for everyone. She is currently working on her first graphic novel. When Josephine isn't drawing or holding workshops with children, she likes to relax with audiobooks and play with the cat that lives in her yard.